M

EMSWORTH 372364

COUNTY FICTION
STORE

15. APR 1997

23. MAY 1997   26. JUN 08

-7. JUN. 1997   20. OCT

22. JUL. 1997   20/10/98

-9. AUG. 1997

21. AUG. 1997   4 DEC 08

-6. NOV. 1997

12. DEC. 1997

-8. JAN. 1998

HOWICK.

C.L. 69
27. FEB. 1998

43/1

HAMPSHIRE COUNTY LIBRARY
WITHDRAWN

F   TOWERS

C011894837

D1424277

This book is d   te shown
above; it may   served by
another reader, be renewed by personal application, post, or
telephone, quoting this date and details of the book.

HAMPSHIRE COUNTY LIBRARY

M

THE RAKE'S COMPANION

Regina Towers

Since her Papa's death, when she was eighteen, Faith Duncan had kept body and soul together by serving as nurse-companion to a string of querulous old ladies. But nothing could have prepared her for the imperious Countess of Moorshead Castle — and her two handsome nephews at war for the fortune to come at her death. Mr Felix Kinston and the brooding Earl of Moorshead were blood brothers and mortal enemies. And Faith Duncan was the prize in between.

THE RAKE'S COMPANION

Regina Towers

Curley Publishing, Inc.
South Yarmouth, Ma.

Library of Congress Cataloging-in-Publication Data

Towers, Regina.
  The rake's companion / Regina Towers.
    p. cm.
  1. Large type books. I. Title.
  [PR6070.O86R34 1990]
  823'.914—dc20
  ISBN 0–7927–0241–7 (lg. print)   89–38827
  ISBN 0–7927–0237–9 (pbk.: lg. print)   CIP

Copyright © 1980 by Regina Towers

All rights reserved. No part of this book may be used or reproduced in any manner without written permission except in the case of brief quotations embodied in critical articles and reviews.

Published in Large Print by arrangement with Donald MacCampbell, Inc. in the United States, Canada, the U.K. and British Commonwealth.

Distributed in Great Britain, Ireland and the Commonwealth by CHIVERS LIBRARY SERVICES LIMITED, Bath BA1 3HB, England.

HAMPSHIRE COUNTY LIBRARY

F

0792702379

C011694837

Printed in Great Britain

for those who love
regardless of shadows

Chapter 1

The Yorkshire countryside was soaked in late summer rain. It burdened every tree and hedgerow and laid the grass low with its weight. It ran in little rivulets down the sides of the closed carriage and streamed off the coachman and the patiently trotting horses. The coachman, cursing under his breath, damned the country, the weather, and his employer, Mr. Felix Kingston.

Inside the carriage, Faith Duncan tucked a wisp of chestnut hair back into the coil that lay against her neck and sighed. There was something dreadfully gloomy about the countryside in this weather. It looked lonely and uninhabited. And the closer they approached Moorshead Castle, the more desolate and dreary it appeared. Of course, the rain did not help matters. Probably when the sun was shining and the heather could be seen all abloom this was a lovely place. But now everything was sodden and gray.

Well, she told herself as she shifted wearily on the velvet squabs, she had been forewarned about the location. Mr. Felix Kingston had told her that Moorshead was a lonely place,

1

far from any neighbours, and that she could not expect much company there.

Suddenly Faith felt the carriage come to a halt. Peering out the window through the gathering dusk and rain, she could just make out the castle. Her heart leaped up in her throat. Never in her life had she seen such a grim and foreboding structure. Just the look of it made her feel ill with apprehension and fright.

The carriage had stopped at the bottom of a steep, rocky road, evidently so that the coachman could open the rusty iron gate that barred the narrow way. The wind beat harshly against the sides of the carriage and a single gaunt pine tree bowed before its force. Tired and chilled as she already was, Faith felt an additional chill; it seemed to settle into her very bones.

In the dim light the castle loomed, cold and heartless as the huge ledge of jutting rock that served as its foundation. Four great towers stood stark against the evening sky, suggesting to the frightened Faith some sort of terrible prison. And about the whole of the place hung a strangeness, a sinister quality that gave her a most distressing feeling. She shuddered and pulled her cloak closer about her. Perhaps she had made a mistake coming so far from London, to a place she knew so little of. And yet, what else could she have done?

In her memory Faith returned to those dreadful days in the city. Since her Papa's death when she was eighteen she had kept body and soul together by serving as nurse-companion to querulous old ladies. She had never known the mother who died giving her birth; she *had* known love and affection from the housekeeper Trilby and her governess Menton. But they were long gone out of her life, for Papa's death had left her without any substance whatsoever. And so she had become companion to the first in a string of old ladies, in the same fashion as she had found this position, by answering an advertisement in the *Times*.

Her last employer had been a vile-tempered, nasty old shrew; as her companion, however, Faith had at least been fed and clothed. But Mrs. Petrie's death had left her completely alone and friendless, with very little money. In the tiny cubbyhole of a room that she found, she had diligently read the *Times*. But positions were few.

All of London was caught up in the coming coronation. At last the Prince Regent was to become king. He was perhaps not the best of men, but the people had not had a coronation

3

for many long years and they were determined to enjoy it.

It seemed to Faith that she was the only person in London who had other, more important, concerns. She could think only of her dwindling supply of money and the disaster that awaited her when it was gone.

And then she had seen the advertisement. At first she found it a little suspicious.

A young woman is needed for nurse-companion to an elderly lady. Those applying should have no other responsibilities and be prepared to leave London immediately. Ask for Mr. Felix Kingston at the Inn of the Three Swans between the hours of 4 and 6.

Faith told herself that she could at least go for an interview. Certainly there could be no harm in that. And her money was going so fast. She must not let any opportunity escape her.

So she presented herself at the appointed time and place. The innkeeper gazed at her curiously, but she was confident that she looked entirely respectable in her cloak of drab brown and her dull serviceable bonnet.

The innkeeper seemed satisfied, too, for he sent her to follow a maid to a private room where she was admitted. A mild-looking man, perhaps a little older than her own age of five and twenty, rose from his chair.

"I am Faith Duncan," she said. "I came in answer to your advertisement for a nurse-companion."

The man smiled. "Very good. Do sit down, Miss Duncan."

Faith settled into a chair and he returned to his. "I must tell you something about the position. First, have you a gentleman friend or aged parents?"

Faith shook her head. "No, sir. My Papa was my only relative and he has been dead these seven years."

"And no gentleman friend?" The mild blue eyes settled on her hair, which, although its luxuriance could be restrained in a coil, persisted in being a rich chestnut hue.

"No, sir," Faith replied. "Mrs. Petrie, my previous employer, did not allow her servants to have callers."

"I see. That's too bad."

"I assure you, sir, it mattered little to me. I have no hopes of marriage and look only for a position in which I may be of service."

"And you do not mind residing away from London – in a somewhat isolated area?"

Faith permitted herself a small smile.

"Indeed, sir, living at Mrs. Petrie's *was* living in an isolated area."

"I see. And why are you seeking a new position?"

"Mrs. Petrie departed this world," Faith replied. "And unless I wish shortly to follow her – due to starvation – I must find another position."

Mr. Kingston smiled in acknowledgment of her humor. "The Yorkshire moors are wild," he cautioned. "There are few servants in the castle – and none your age."

"That is of no concern to me," replied Faith. "But what of the woman whose companion I am to be?"

"The Countess is ailing. It's her age, no doubt. And isolated as she is she needs proper care and attention – something her old servants cannot give her."

"I see." Faith frowned thoughtfully. "I believe I am quite qualified for this position and I am not bothered by any of the things you have mentioned to me."

"Fine," Mr. Kingston smiled at her, his mild blue eyes reflecting his pleasure. "Be here with your belongings on Tuesday next. I shall send a closed carriage for you."

"That is most thoughtful, sir. But I can come on the mail coach."

"Nonsense. If you are jostled about in that

horrid coach for hours on end – and with the low-class company one usually finds there –" He wrinkled his nose in disgust. "You will be useless to my aunt if you arrive in an exhausted condition. And that is what the mail coach will do to you. You come here Tuesday next at eight in the morning and the innkeeper will show you the proper carriage. We will consider your duties further after you arrive at Moorshead."

"Moorshead?"

"Yes, Moorshead Castle. It's very old – actually a fortified fifteenth-century manor house. But it's called the castle. No one knows now if it got its name from the rock on which it sits, jutting out over the countryside, which looks like a Moor's head, or from the fact that it sits at the 'head' of the moor lands. But no matter. It's a grim, drafty old place, but really rather comfortable."

"Yes, sir," replied Faith. "I am sure I shall find it so."

"Good. Then I shall see you when you arrive."

The clatter of hooves brought Faith abruptly back to the present. The horses had started up the steep, rocky road. Looking up at the castle, Faith could see no lights anywhere. The whole place looked desolate and foreboding. Again she felt a wave of fear.

7

What if the castle were deserted? What if she had come this long way for nothing?

But common sense soon asserted itself. Faith gave herself a scolding. The steady beating of the rain on the roof of the carriage, the dampness and chill of the long tedious journey, the apprehension of going into a new employment, all these were working against her.

Of course there would be someone in the castle. They were expecting her. After all, Mr. Kingston had sent the carriage for her. She had never been one to give in to panic or this kind of senseless fear. If she had, she would have been lost long ago. For there had been some bad moments in the seven years since Papa's death, some very bad moments.

Now, as the carriage drew nearer, moving slowly up the road, she saw lights appear in several places and breathed a sigh of relief. The journey had been a long, weary one and she would be glad to wash and have a bite to eat. She had not slept well in the inn the night before and the thought of a comfortable bed was even more satisfying. She felt as though she had been jounced and jiggled into a thousand bruises. Undoubtedly Mr. Kingston was right. By mail coach the trip would have been a nightmare. Closed up with noisome or aggravating travelers for several days she would have been twice as weary. Now, with just a good night's sleep she would be in fine shape again.

The carriage clattered to a halt before the great scarred door of the castle. Faith suppressed a shiver. All her life had been spent in London and, although she had certainly seen castles before, she had never seen one in such an eerie setting.

Moments later she found herself and the valise which held all her worldly possessions standing in the great hall. The Countess must be very plump in the pocket, thought Faith. The great hall was hung with paintings and tapestries that appeared quite costly – and old.

The butler, an aged retainer with a rotund figure and a long dismal face that contrasted oddly with each other, left her standing while he went to inform Mr. Kingston of her arrival.

The vastness of the great hall made Faith uneasy and she occupied herself with looking at the paintings, some of which were portraits. One in particular held her attention. It was of a dark handsome man with hard black eyes and a stubbornly set jaw. The rich court clothes that he wore marked him as an aristocrat, but, thought Faith, even in a peasant's rags his noble blood would be

9

visible. The man held his head arrogantly, as though contemptuous of the world upon which he gazed, a world quite beneath his touch.

Perhaps this had been one of the late Earl's ancestors, Faith thought. Perhaps even the one who had built this castle. The man had a decided piratical look about him.

A small cough behind her made her turn. The rotund butler was regarding her gloomily. "Mr. Kingston will see you now in the drawing room. Follow me."

Faith, seeing that the little man made no move toward her valise, stooped for it herself.

"That is unnecessary," said the butler. "I will have it taken to your room."

"Thank you."

The drawing room, Faith saw as she entered it, was also elegantly done, though rather old-fashioned. By the hearth, where a fire blazed brightly, sat Mr. Felix Kingston, his mild blue eyes smiling. "Ah, Miss Duncan, you made the trip successfully, I see."

Faith nodded. "Yes, Mr. Kingston. And I thank you again for the closed carriage. I have not traveled much, but I can see how much more comfortable that was than the mail coach."

"But you are still cold through and bone weary, I've no doubt." Mr. Kingston motioned to her. "Come, have a seat by the fire. Spacks, some tea and cakes for Miss Duncan."

"You are most kind," said Faith gratefully as she sank into a chair. "I did find the journey a weary one," she admitted. "But then, I am not used to traveling."

Mr. Kingston smiled. "I believe that you have led a rather secluded life as nurse-companion."

Faith nodded. "I have, but it is a way of life. And I must live."

Mr. Kingston nodded sympathetically. "So must we all."

Faith thought that her eyes must have reflected something because her new employer suddenly chuckled. "I see that you are among those who believe that the aristocracy *has* no problems."

Faith, about to deny this, realized its truth and smiled. "I do not have many dealings with the aristocracy," she replied. "So I suppose I am ill-equipped to make such judgments. My previous employers have not been titled."

Felix Kingston smiled again, that friendly smile which made Faith feel quite comfortable. "Although you have not said so, I gather that your previous employers were rather hard to live with."

Faith did not deny this.

"You will find the Countess a little querulous at times, but basically she is a good-hearted old soul. It's unfortunate that she is so cozened by my brother."

"Your brother?" This was the first Faith had heard of such a person.

"Yes, my brother is the Earl of Moorshead – and my aunt's heir. Sometimes I think he would not mind should Aunt's departure be hast –" He stopped suddenly. "You must forgive me, Miss Duncan. My brother is an unscrupulous man, well-noted for taking whatever strikes his fancy whether it be women, land, or . . ."

Mr. Kingston's fair boyish face puckered into a frown. "But enough – I have only suspicions, no facts. I must plead with you, though, to keep your eyes open."

"Of course." Faith suppressed a little shiver. What sort of position was this? Far away from the city and now with intimations of something sinister on the part of Mr. Kingston's brother. Then common sense asserted itself again. In an old castle like this one's imagination was apt to run riot. Probably the Earl and his brother did not get along well. Many brothers did not. And so they were suspicious of each other.

"Ah, here comes Spacks with your tea and cakes."

12

Faith, raising the delicate cup to her lips, wished for a hearty chunk of bread and meat. But years of service in the vagaries of rich old ladies had accustomed her to subsisting on whatever was put before her and so she ate one cake and reached for another.

"My aunt has already gone to sleep for the night. She is recovering from a strange illness which the doctor could not recognize."

It was plain to Faith that Mr. Kingston did not believe that the illness was a natural one. "The old are often subject to strange ailments," she said calmly. "I am sure I can make her quite comfortable."

Felix Kingston smiled at her warmly. "I'm sure you can, Miss Duncan. I recognized that the moment I saw you. You appear to be a very warm, compassionate person."

Faith did not know how to reply to this. Certainly there was nothing wrong with hiring a warm, compassionate person as a nurse-companion to one's aunt. And there was nothing wrong in smiling on that person warmly. In fact, Faith decided that she liked Mr. Felix Kingston; he seemed a reasonable, kindhearted man.

Of course, being the practical young woman that she was, she realized that her long years of residence in maiden establishments had not left her well equipped for dealing with gentlemen. But there was nothing in Mr. Kingston's behavior at which to take umbrage, and it was exceedingly pleasant after years of being yelled at and scolded for little or no cause by shrewish old women to be spoken to kindly and treated with respect by a young gentleman.

Faith finished her second cake. "Please tell me more about the establishment here."

Mr. Kingston regarded her kindly. "You have seen Spacks, Aunt's butler. Deevers, the housekeeper, is also old. They have been with Aunt for many years. There are also a few maids, the cook, and some servants in the stables. Actually, Aunt subsists with a minimum of staff. A great part of the castle is closed off and unused."

Faith nodded. "I see."

"I reside here at the present because of Aunt's illness," Mr. Kingston continued. "You will also meet my brother." His bland face registered dislike. "And a great-niece of my aunt's – Lady Clarisse. She is of about your age and rather a shrew, I fear. Currently she is on the scramble for my brother, because he is the heir. He already has the title, of course, and the late Earl's funds, but Aunt's jointure was quite large. The late Earl was rather enamored of her when they married. They say she was quite a beauty, then."

14

He smiled. "But you must be exhausted from your journey. Time enough to learn about the vagaries of this family as you become one of us. I will have Spacks take you to your room."

"You are most kind," Faith replied, rising from her chair and thinking with gratitude of a soft bed.

Mr. Kingston rose, too, and covered her hand with his. He seemed very close to her and Faith was suddenly uncomfortable. Men were dangerous creatures; she had been warned about them continually. She wished to withdraw her hand but did not quite know how to do so. Perhaps if she turned to go ... In her confusion, however, she caught her toe on the leg of the chair and found herself suddenly propelled into Mr. Felix Kingston's arms.

"Oh, sir!" breathed Faith in embarrassment. "Excuse me, sir." A sudden noise from the doorway caused her to color up. It certainly would not help her with the servants to be seen in such a position. She did not look toward the door. Better to pretend the butler had not seen.

Mr. Kingston set her on her feet and smiled, but not before she had realized, much to her dismay, that being held in a man's arms was rather a pleasant sensation.

15

Her new employer continued to smile at her. "I hope you will be happy with us and consider this your home."

Faith found herself coloring up again. "Thank you," she murmured. "I shall try to do that."

As she followed Spacks out into the hall, she heard the closing of the great front door. "Has someone come in?" she asked. It was better to act as if nothing untoward had happened.

The butler's smile was not particularly friendly. " 'Twas his lordship you heard. He was just going out."

"I see." Faith kept her voice even, hiding her relief. It was really better that she did not have to face the rakish Earl at this time. She had had quite enough for one day.

Then she was following Spacks up the great stone staircase and down a long dark corridor where shadows hovered in every corner. The candles in Spack's candelabra flickered in the draft, but the round little man did not seem disturbed. "This," he said, stopping before a great door, "is to be your room. The Countess's is the next one on. The fire's been lit and your valise is inside."

"Thank you." Faith turned the knob and stepped into the room. The fire blazing brightly on the hearth was the one real spot of light in the room. On a stand near the bed, a massive old piece hung with brocade curtains, stood a lone candle. Faith suppressed a shiver. The room was a mass of shadows.

She took a deep breath, stepped in, and shut the door. She had few choices, she told herself, actually none at all. This *was* to be her home and she must make the best of it. There was nothing but a few pence in her pocket – the full extent of her monetary resources.

With a sigh she opened the valise and began putting away her belongings, a procedure that did not take a great deal of time. Her worldly belongings, thought Faith with a wry smile – the accumulation of five and twenty years of living. Not much to look at. But then, she was lucky to be alive at all. If she had been forced into the streets, like so many of London's young girls, she might by now be dead. No, considering the tremendous odds confronting her, she had been fortunate to survive.

With another sigh she slipped out of her drab brown dress and into a much-mended nightdress. If all went well here, perhaps she could afford some new clothes. Nothing extravagant, of course, just a few new gowns, perhaps even one of a lighter shade than her dull browns and grays. And a new nightdress and chemise or two.

She smiled thoughtfully as she crawled into

17

the old bed and pulled up the covers. In spite of its isolation and its shadows, life at Moorshead Castle might well be very good, very good indeed.

Chapter 2

Faith, waking early the next morning, gazed at the ceiling of the great bed. Here she was in Moorshead Castle in far Yorkshire. And soon she would be meeting the old Countess.

Faith stretched. The bed was quite comfortable and she had been nice and warm under the comforter. It appeared that life here was going to be considerably better than it had been with Mrs. Petrie. It was strange that rich old ladies should be so niggardly with their money considering that they had so little time left in which to spend it.

But long ago she had been forced to concede that there was no understanding her employers. The best defense was an unfailing cheerfulness and compliance. By dint of hard practice Faith had managed to subdue an orginally volatile temperament and now could face the world with an even complacency.

She chose one of her few equally drab gowns, washed and dressed, and twisted her rich chestnut hair into a coil. Her stomach, which had not been particularly well cared for in the last few weeks, was complaining audibly at its emptiness. She would just make her way below stairs and see what could be found for breakfast.

The long corridor was dark and shadowed. She would have to get used to shadows, Faith told herself with a shiver, if she were going to be here long. And hopefully she would be.

She made her way down the broad stone staircase and then paused to look around her. Surely there were servants abroad somewhere in this great hulk.

"Have you lost your way?" inquired a deep voice.

Startled, Faith whirled and then her hand flew to her mouth in surprise. Standing before her was an exact replica of the man in the portrait which she had studied the night before.

"You need not look as though you have seen a ghost," the man said sardonically. "I assure you that I am very much flesh and blood. Didn't my dear brother Felix tell you about me?"

Faith could not help staring. "You – you are the Earl?"

"So I have been told," he replied dryly. "But I am not an ogre to eat young women alive."

Faith shook her head. "It is just that you are so like the portrait."

"My revered ancestor," replied the dark brooding man before her. "A pirate and thief. A thoroughly respectable Englishman – of Elizabeth's time."

Faith, still unsure if she was awake or dreaming, took a step closer to the man. "Respectable?" she repeated. "I find your standards of respectability a little strange."

The Earl gave her a sharp glance. "It appears to me that one of your ilk had best leave considerations of respectability aside. Come, I will share my breakfast tea with you. Lady Clarisse is a late riser and seems to have forgotten that we have an engagement to ride this morning."

As Faith followed him into what was obviously the library she felt an insane urge to pinch herself. This seemed more like a dream than reality. And what could he have meant by the comment about one of her ilk?

The Earl gestured to a chair by the fire. Faith took it; she felt suddenly chilled through, somehow. That sinister air she had perceived before seemed to hang about this man.

She still felt in a kind of daze. To be living in a great castle, smiled at by Mr. Felix Kingston, and now – invited to breakfast by the Earl!

He put a cup of tea in her hand – another fragile cup, she saw, and glanced down at her quizzically. "And is Moorshead Castle all you were led to believe?"

Faith found she could not take her glance away from the darkly piercing eyes that gazed into her own. "I – I have not seen much of it," she replied, trying not to color up under the scrutiny of those probing eyes. Surely all gentlemen did not look at women like this – with so much open speculation in their glance.

"Well, there is not much to see. You may go up on the cliffs and look out over the moors. Or if you are foolhardy, you may even wander there. Do you ride?"

Faith shook her head. "No. Nurse-companions do not have much time for riding."

The Earl laughed. It was a harsh, brutal sound – one that sent shivers down her spine. "I suppose your employers preferred to keep you in seclusion."

"Yes, they did," replied Faith, wondering why his eyes should rake over her like that, almost as though he meant to rip off her

21

clothes! The color rushed to her face at the thought. She must be imagining it.

"My little brother has an admirable facility for finding companions for Aunt."

Faith set down her cup and got to her feet. "You mean I am not the first?"

The Earl's dark eyes glittered with laughter. "The first? Indeed not! You are perhaps the fifth or sixth."

"The fifth or sixth!"

The Earl bowed in mockery. "More or less."

"The others – what happened to them?"

The Earl took a step nearer, bringing his dark face close to hers. "They could not stand the loneliness here or my Aunt could not stand them."

"But, but I do not understand. If you do not approve of his choices, why didn't you engage someone yourself?"

The Earl shrugged. "I myself did not see the necessity for such a person. Nor did Aunt. But it amuses me to see what Felix turns up. Usually they don't stay long and since *he* pays their wages..." He eyed her suggestively. "Occasionally they are even worth looking at."

Faith found this sort of reasoning rather odd. The Earl was a strange man – mysterious and with a darkness about him that had

22

nothing to do with his physical coloring. She felt the blood rush to her cheeks as he continued to regard her. He seemed excessively close to her and Faith felt a strange rush of weakness.

Suddenly his hand reached out and loosened the coil of her hair so that it fell on her shoulder. "I must admit, though, that the others were not nearly so beautiful, nor as good actresses."

Faith stared in amazement into the dark eyes so near her own. Beautiful? No man had ever called her beautiful before. And why did he think she was an actress?

The Earl smiled sardonically. "I'm sure my brother offered you good wages. He always does. But I will double them."

Faith's mind was in a turmoil. Why, why should he double her wages? She had already promised to do her best for the old Countess. "I – I do not understand," she faltered.

"Of course not," he mocked. "But perhaps you understand this." And while she watched with unbelieving eyes, he buried one hand in her mass of chestnut hair and pulled her into his arms.

For a moment Faith was speechless. Except for her fall into Mr. Kingston's arms, she had not been touched by a man since before her father's death and never then by a man

23

her own age. The shock of it left her momentarily motionless. While her senses were still trying to comprehend the sensations of being encircled by a pair of strong arms, his mouth covered hers. He took her lips brutally, savagely. It was the only kiss Faith had ever known, and for a long moment she was unable to struggle. Indeed, she found her own arms creeping up to circle his neck.

But when he released her mouth and his lips began to travel along the curve of her throat, sanity returned. "Milord! You must release me at once."

The Earl lifted his head. "I have never taken a woman against her will," he declared. "You *were* quite willing a moment ago."

"I – I did not know what you intended," she stammered, completely unnerved by the sight of his face so near her own.

The Earl laughed again, harshly. "You did not *know?*" he mocked. "You stood there with an open invitation in your eyes and you did not know?"

For some strange reason Faith felt compelled to apologize. "I – I have no experience with men, milord. I did not intend to look like that. Truly I didn't."

For a long moment the Earl stared at her, and then he pushed her away roughly, so roughly that she almost fell. "You do your part very well. I could almost believe you."

Faith fought to gather her scattered senses. "Milord, I do not know what misapprehension you are laboring under but I assure you, I am just what I appear to be – a nurse – a nurse-companion hired to attend your aunt."

The Earl smiled cynically. "Of course, of course. We shall discuss the matter no further."

Faith sank into her chair. She longed for some tea to calm her nerves, but she knew she was still too shaken to lift the cup. Whatever had happened to the sane, dull life she was accustomed to leading? Only days ago the most troubling thing in her life had been another worn spot in her chemise. And now she had been smiled upon by one brother and rudely kissed by the other. A world with men in it was extremely unsettling.

She turned so she could observe the Earl's profile. He was gazing morosely into the fire. His hair was very dark with a slight natural curl to it. His eyes, under dark brows, were black and piercing. His nose, high and aristocratic, presided over a mouth whose lines were cruel and hard. How was it, Faith wondered, that a kiss so savage and cruel, so obviously an assault on her senses and an insult to her person, could cause her bones to become limp and make her wish – God forbid – to have that kiss repeated!

Well, she told herself, she had probably made a mistake in letting his lordship know that she was inexperienced, but now that she was forewarned, she would keep her distance from him. He must be one of those rakes that the maids had always whispered about. Faith had never paid much heed to their chatter, but now she could see what made such men succeed. By the time their victims regained their ravaged senses the damage was done.

She was pondering her next move when the clatter of heels was heard in the hall and a woman rushed into the room in a swirl of heavy scent and velvet. "Hugh, my dear, I *am* sorry. That stupid Lucy neglected to wake me. Is it too late for our ride?"

This must be the Lady Clarisse, Faith thought, as the woman came to a halt inches away from the Earl. She was a lovely woman. Her sable hair was piled high under the little velvet riding cap and the body that was sheathed in matching red velvet was voluptuous and well cared for. She pressed the Earl's arm with gloved fingers. "Come, Hugh, answer me. Say I am not too late."

The Earl carefully disengaged her fingers. "I fear that we will have to postpone our ride, my dear. For a little at least. In your hurry you did not notice Aunt's new companion, Miss . . ."

"Duncan," replied Faith, finding herself the uncomfortable recipient of a frosty stare from a pair of icy gray eyes.

The eyes turned back to the Earl and softened. "But Hugh, dearest, I got up this early just for our ride."

"It won't take me that long," his lordship replied. "Just pour yourself a cup of tea."

The Lady Clarisse's lovely red mouth puckered in a pout, but she made no further comment.

The Earl turned to Faith. "Come, my aunt should be awake by now. I am curious to see her reaction to you."

Numbly Faith rose from her chair and followed the Earl from the library and up the broad stone stairs. Again she was conscious of an irrational urge to pinch herself. Surely this could not be reality.

But the Earl's broad shoulders beneath his tautly stretched coat looked very real. And certainly she could not have imagined the feel of his arms around her or of his lips on hers. No, this must be real, but it was a strangely different world than that in which she was accustomed to living – that world in which the only men had been aged butlers and grooms.

The Earl turned and moved down the

corridor past her door. "I trust you were comfortable last night."

"Yes, indeed," answered Faith automatically. "But tell me, milord, what ails your aunt?"

The Earl turned blazing dark eyes on her. "The doctor has been unable to arrive at a diagnosis. I am sure, however, that *you* will soon discover it."

Faith was about to ask what he meant by this, but before she could open her mouth the Earl had turned the knob and was propelling her into the room.

The curtains had not yet been opened and Faith could not see well in the dimness. "Is that you, Hugh?" came a querulous voice from the bed.

"Indeed it is, Aunt. I have brought your new companion."

"For mercy's sake, Hugh. Don't tell me Felix has engaged another of those creatures."

The Earl dropped Faith's elbow and strode across the room to throw open the curtains. The sunlight pouring in caused Faith to blink.

"I am not sure about this *creature*, but I think perhaps you may like her."

"I may *what?* Come here, girl, let me see you."

Obediently Faith approached the great bed.

28

This kind of conversation did not trouble her. In the last seven years she had faced many a harridan – faced them and survived. She drew nearer to the Earl's side, where the bed's curtains were open.

"What's your name, girl?" demanded the little woman who was almost lost in the great heap of pillows that supported her.

"I am Faith Duncan and I have come to be your companion, if you wish me to."

A pair of piercing black eyes, very like the Earl's, gazed at her inquisitively. Faith did not flush or quiver under their gaze. She was used to being surveyed by angry old ladies.

There was a long moment of silence in the room and then a chuckle issued from the old woman's wrinkled throat. "Hugh, my boy, I believe you are right. This one *is* different." She shot the Earl a sharp look. "I see that hair, Hugh. Now you stay away from this girl. I think Felix made a mistake. He's not a good judge of character, you know."

It was the Earl's turn to chuckle. "You're right about Felix, Aunt. But you should know –" he turned burning eyes on Faith, eyes that made a strange sensation travel down her spine, "that forbidding me has never kept me from something I wanted."

The old woman shook her finger at him. "You behave yourself, Hugh. You hear me?"

29

"I hear you, Aunt." The Earl was still smiling sardonically. "But I make no promises. At any rate, Miss Duncan is undoubtedly able to take care of herself."

Faith, remembering the ferocity of that kiss, was not quite so sure of that. But of one thing she *was* certain. She would keep this strange man at a distance. After all, hadn't his brother practically accused him of wanting to hasten his aunt's death? That did seem rather strange, especially in view of the good feeling that seemed to exist between the Earl and his aunt, but Faith reserved judgment. Perhaps Mr. Felix knew his brother better than his aunt did.

The Earl kissed the Countess's cheek. "Miss Duncan has the room next to yours. Right now I must leave you. Lady Clarisse is waiting for me to take her for a ride."

The old lady sniffed again. "Is that flibbertigibbet still hanging around here? I warn you, my boy, she's after you. Clarisse was always one with an eye for a title."

The Earl chuckled. "My dear Aunt, is it possible that your illness has affected your eyesight? Have you forgotten that I have sufficient personal attractions to induce a partiality for me in a woman's heart?"

The Countess stuck her tongue out at him. "Hugh, my boy, you were too long in

London. It has affected your senses."

"Come, Aunt," chuckled his lordship. "We will ask an impartial observer. Miss Duncan, I appeal to you. Do you find that my physical attributes are attractive to a young woman?"

Faith found herself coloring up. "I – I am sure I don't know, milord. I have little experience of men."

"Of course." His lordship's eyes raked over her. "I had forgotten."

"Hugh! Go to Clarisse and leave my companion alone! I like the girl. Now don't be harassing her."

The Earl bowed. "Yes, Aunt. You're right. She's too much of an innocent for the likes of me." And with another ironic glance at Faith his lordship left the room.

"Come closer, Faith," said the old lady.

Obediently Faith moved toward the great bed.

"Do you always wear your hair loose like that?" the Countess demanded suddenly.

Caught by surprise, Faith flushed.

"Don't tell me that scamp has been at you already."

Faith found herself unable to dissemble. "Yes," she murmured, "but, but he took me by surprise."

The old lady in the bed grimaced. "Bring a chair over here and sit down. I want to hear about your life before you came here."

As in a dream, Faith did as she was told. She had never confided in anyone before; actually she had little to confide. The tale of her life with her various employers was quite short and very dull. She, of course, omitted telling of the Earl's kiss. His aunt could only blame *her* for that. "I – I have seen little of the world," she concluded. "And I did not invite the Earl's attention. Truly I didn't."

"Of course, you didn't." The Countess's eyes gleamed at her. "No woman needs to *invite* Hugh's attention. He is always ready to bestow it."

Faith frowned. "Then it was not my fault?"

The Countess laughed. "Of course not. Don't be a ninny. Hugh is a rake. He has an eye for the petticoat line. That's all."

"And you laugh at this?" asked Faith.

The old lady's eyes softened. "I know I shouldn't, but the lad's so like his uncle – my departed Henry. I really can't get angry with the boy. His smile disarms me, you see. It's like my Henry's come alive again. But you needn't fear Hugh. He will not pursue a woman who shuns him. And for your own sake I advise you to do so."

"Of course," Faith realized that this was the obvious thing to do. She had no business trifling with an Earl.

"Let me fluff up your pillows, milady. And then you must have some breakfast."

The old lady wrinkled her nose. "I only want my cup of chocolate."

Faith shook her head. "Milady, my job is to see that you are restored to health and to do that you must eat. Now, what will you eat?"

The Countess glared at her stubbornly, but Faith returned the stare quite evenly. The old face crinkled into a smile. "All right, Faith. I'll have a boiled egg and a piece of toasted bread."

"Yes, milady." Faith smiled. She and the Countess would deal together famously. She was sure of it.

As she bustled around the room straightening this and adjusting that, her smile faded. She could deal with the Countess and with the kindhearted Mr. Felix Kingston with the smiling blue eyes, but could she deal with that dark, brooding man whose gaze caused her to blush and whose kiss still tingled on her bruised lips? And what of the animosity between the brothers and the suspicion of something dreadful that hung over the old castle?

She straightened her shoulders. She would deal with whatever happened. To leave this place was patently impossible. She had no funds and besides, the thought of leaving the Countess if she were in trouble was quite foreign to Faith's nature. She simply must make the best of what she had. That was all there was to do.

Chapter 3

The day sped by for Faith. She tended to the Countess and brought the room into order. That afternoon while the Countess slept Faith mended another worn place in a chemise. She was taking the last stitch, neatly and carefully, as Trilby had taught her so long ago, when the old woman in the bed stirred. "Faith, where are you?"

Faith rose hastily and went to the bed, trailing the mended chemise. "I am doing some mending," she said, "over by the window where the light is better."

The Countess's eyes lit on the worn chemise. "I see. Come, let that go for a spell. Ring for Deevers."

Obediently Faith pulled on the bell to summon the servant.

"Now go find that new French novel Clarisse brought me. It's around here somewhere. A lot of hogwash, of course. But it passes the time."

"Yes, milady."

Faith had found the novel and was pulling a chair close to the bed when the door opened. "Yes, milady?" A small, wizened woman appeared in the doorway.

"Deevers, this is Faith Duncan, my new companion."

The housekeeper's face remained impassive. Faith had to suppress a shiver. Everyone around here seemed so cold.

"Deevers, I like Faith. She belongs here."

A smile suddenly appeared on the housekeeper's face and Faith's apprehension vanished. "Yes, milady."

"And Deevers, I have some material around here for chemises and nightgowns. Find it and bring it up."

The housekeeper's smile grew even warmer. "Yes, milady. Right soon."

The Countess smiled happily at Faith. "You can make yourself some new things."

Faith felt a sudden lump in her throat. "Oh, my lady. You are very kind."

"Nonsense! A woman must have clothes. The stuff will simply rot if we don't use it."

"Yes, milady. Thank you." What a kindhearted person the Countess was, thought Faith. Surely her nephews could only wish to keep her with them as long as possible.

She settled in the chair. "Your nephews must be pleased that you are recovering."

The Countess cast her a strange look. "Felix and Hugh do not deal well together," she said.

Faith nodded. "I surmised as much."

"I suppose it is not so unusual. Hugh is a strong man – very attractive to the ladies. And Felix..." The Countess shook her head. "Felix is weak. Easily influenced. I fear for that boy. But I promised his mother I'd do my best for him. She was a lovely girl and she befriended me. It was a shame she died so young."

Faith found this conversation a little startling. But further consideration made her pause. She supposed that compared with his lordship Mr. Felix could be called weak. But, she told herself firmly, there were some things to be said for a mild-mannered, kind man who did not attack a woman with savage kisses, a man who knew how to speak in a civilized fashion without constant irony and innuendo.

"Faith! Faith! Did you hear me?"

Faith was called back to reality. "I'm sorry, milady. I was woolgathering."

The Countess smiled. "I was telling you about Clarisse. I'm sorry to say she comes from *my* side of the family. My sister always gave the girl everything she wanted. Unfortunately, my sister's husband was not a man of great substance, at least not enough to satisfy Clarisse. And she has gone through the money left her by her first husband – a man twice her age. And now she is looking again for a husband with money and a title."

"His..." Faith bit her tongue. It was entirely unlike her to give away her thoughts like this.

The old woman nodded. "Yes, she's after his lordship. Oh, do not look so distressed, my child, Hugh is four and thirty and old enough to take care of himself. No woman will ever bring Hugh to heel – at least no woman like Clarisse."

Faith frowned. "I don't understand. I saw her. She – she is very beautiful."

"Of course she is. That is not the point at all. Hugh has seen many beautiful women in his day and had all of them he wanted, no doubt. No, this is a matter of character. Hugh will never lose his heart to a woman of the world. They are too much like him." She smiled fondly. "If the boy ever falls top-over-tail, it will be to a young innocent. That's how it was with me and my Henry."

The Countess's face wrinkled in a smile. "My Henry. Oh, he was the talk of all London and six and thirty the year I came out. But he fell. He fell just as hard as any half-grown moonling."

"How – how did you do it?" asked Faith, and flushed at the temerity of her question.

The Countess smiled again. "I did it by loving him," she said. "I was only eighteen and innocent as a child. But the moment I saw him I knew. I knew that I would marry Henry or never marry anyone."

"And were you happy?" asked Faith gently.

"Oh, yes," said the Countess. "Henry was a marvellous man. And he reformed. From the moment we were promised he never touched another woman."

Faith's face must have reflected her disbelief.

"It's true, my dear. We lived in each other's pockets. Yes, they were very good years. I never regretted my choice. If ever Hugh falls, it will be in like fashion."

"He's not likely to meet any such young woman here," said Faith, finding it difficult to believe that the arrogant Earl would ever give up chasing women.

The Countess sighed. "No, I suppose not. And I did want to see the boy settled before I ... Well, at least Clarisse won't get him. I am sure of that. Now, read me some more of that hogwash until it's time for you to dress for dinner."

"But I will eat here with you."

The old woman shook her head. "Nonsense, I am mistress here. You must have some company besides mine. You will go stale otherwise and be of no use to me either."

There came a soft tap on the door. Faith laid aside the unopened novel and went to open it. Mr. Felix stood there, smiling apologetically. "I have come to speak to Aunt," he said.

Faith nodded. "Just a moment, please." She crossed the room to report, "Mr. Felix is here."

The old woman frowned. "Tell him to come in."

Faith returned to the door. "Come in, sir."

As Mr. Felix advanced across the room, Faith moved toward her own door. "Don't go," said the Countess crisply. "Felix is merely making a duty call and will be leaving shortly. Isn't that so, Felix?"

Faith saw him raise his hand helplessly and shrug. "My dear Aunt, you know I don't wish to distress you. If you want me to make my visit short, I shall certainly do so. I merely came to see how you are getting along?"

"I am my usual irascible self," said the Countess crisply. "Now run along and do whatever it is you waste your time doing.

"Oh, there is one thing." She looked at him with bright eyes. "Thank you for finding Faith."

Mr. Felix smiled expansively. "You're quite welcome, Aunt, I'm sure. My only desire is to make life easier for you."

There was no reply to this and the Countess merely waved him out. As Faith shut the door behind him she marveled at the Countess's treatment of the brothers. Mr. Felix was by far the kinder, more considerate of the two, and yet she favored his lordship.

"Read," said the Countess. "Sometimes I think he comes to see me merely because he knows it riles me so. Come, read me some more of that foolishness."

And so Faith dutifully began to read, and when the bell announced that it was time to dress, she went obediently to her room and freshened up for dinner. She had no dress suitable to change into, but she twisted her hair back into its coil before she moved down the shadowy hall and descended the great stone staircase.

In the dining room she found Mr. Felix Kingston waiting. He smiled at her approach. "I am glad that Aunt is pleased with you." He beamed. "I'm very glad. She has been very difficult lately."

Faith did not reply to this. She did not think it proper to discuss the Countess's disposition.

Kingston sighed. "I suppose she told you about the others. I simply could not seem to please her. I do not understand why. All my life it has been like this." His round face saddened. "When we were children she always favored my brother."

Faith could find nothing to say to this. It must have been a very painful experience for the boy, she thought. She offered Mr. Kingston a consoling smile.

He seemed to brighten. "But she does like you. For once I have done something right. She really does like you."

"Yes," replied Faith, returning his smile. "I like her too."

Kingston frowned. "You met my brother?"

Faith nodded. "I was looking for my breakfast."

"My brother is a strange man." He sighed. "I do not understand him."

Faith did not find this at all unusual. A man with his lordship's rakish tastes must be anathema to a man of Mr. Kingston's placid nature.

He passed a hand over his face. "In London

41

– his reputation. You must understand how difficult it is for me. A man of my kind, with a brother like that." He sighed plaintively.

"I can quite appreciate your distress," said Faith softly.

"Yes, yes." Kingston covered her hand with his. "You have a warm and understanding heart."

He drew her arm through his and moved toward the dining table. The great oak table that had once held many people was set so that the four of them used only one end.

Faith flushed as his lordship entered with Lady Clarisse on his arm. She had never been one to consider clothes; there had been little need of that in the establishments where she had previously worked. But even the most beautiful woman might have quailed at being in the same room with Lady Clarisse. The jet black hair cascaded over one white shoulder. The sheer muslin gown clung to a figure that had no match anywhere. Lady Clarisse raised soft gray eyes to the Earl's face. Momentarily, as those eyes had swept over Faith they had turned chill. She wondered how they could change so quickly. But perhaps that was the way the members of the *ton* behaved. To think that if her Mama had not died as she had, she too would have been a member of that elite group.

With effort she forced herself to smile. She would not bow before the Lady Clarisse, however much she might feel her inferior in looks.

The Earl smiled at her, that lazy smile that did not reach his eyes. "Good evening, Miss Duncan."

"Good evening, milord." Faith, the thought of that savage kiss searing her memory, found it difficult to meet his lordship's eyes, but she did so. She would not be cowed by any of them. She was resolved about that.

And so they seated themselves at the table. Faith found herself on Mr. Kingston's right and across from his lordship. At first it was disconcerting, but as the food began to appear she forgot her nervousness. Such sumptuous meals had not come her way in many long years and she devoted herself to eating with a will.

Once she looked up to find his lordship's eyes regarding her quizzically. "I collect that they did not set much of a table in your previous establishment," he observed dryly.

Faith flushed but refused to be cowed. "You are quite right, milord. My previous employers were usually noted for their frugality. At least where I was concerned."

The Earl's eyes regarded her coolly and

arrogantly, and Faith felt a stirring of anger. "The results of their frugality are not unattractive," he commented.

For a moment Faith was silent. He was arrogant even in his compliments – if that was how his statement was to be taken. "I have had little time or inclination to consider attractiveness," she replied. "A position such as mine calls for dedication to my employer."

The Earl's black eyes lost their lazy arrogance and turned cold and hard. "Of course. Dedication to your employer must be uppermost in your mind."

"Of course," echoed Faith automatically, wondering why such a simple statement should anger him. What a strange man the Earl was! And why should he send such a peculiar glance to his brother?

Faith sighed. Now that she had finally found a place where she might be happy in serving why must these two so complicate matters? Men! she thought to herself. Perhaps those old ladies such as Mrs. Petrie had been right. Perhaps men *were* unfathomable, almost another species, better shunned for one's own safety.

Well, she could keep out of the way of the arrogant Earl as much as possible, but she could not avoid him entirely. Nor could she avoid Mr. Felix. In fact, she did not wish to. The Countess might be attracted to self-willed rakes like her beloved Henry, but Faith preferred a man with a kind, warm smile. She cast a sidelong look at Mr. Felix and found him beaming at her approvingly. Lowering her eyes, she returned her attention to her meal. Yes, she preferred a civilized man anytime.

Across the table Lady Clarisse laughed, a silver sound that rang artificially in Faith's ears. As Lady Clarisse leaned close to his lordship, touching his arm familiarly, Faith remembered the Countess's words. The old lady might believe that her niece had no chance with his lordship, but Lady Clarisse herself was certainly not of that opinion. And Faith, seeing the ease with which she plied her charms, could not but wonder that his lordship could withstand her. But then, Faith realized that she herself knew little of the ways of the *ton*. Perhaps many London ladies were equally attractive – and accessible.

"Have you warned our new resident about the ghost?" Lady Clarisse asked suddenly.

Mr. Felix shook his head. "No, it's not the time of month for her yet."

Faith, with her fork halfway to her mouth, looked from one to the other. "You have a ghost?"

"Yes, indeed," declared his lordship. "She

appears around the time of the full moon."

"I see." Faith was plainly skeptical. "And who is she supposed to be the ghost *of?*"

The Earl laughed, a harsh, brutal sound that somehow reminded her of that savage kiss. "Perhaps you noticed the picture of my ancestor in the entrance hall?"

Faith put down her fork and nodded. He knew she had seen that painting.

"The story goes that he had a recalcitrant wife, one who refused to submit to his wishes and sit quietly by while he indulged in amorous pursuits. And so one night in a fit of drunken rage he is supposed to have pushed her over the cliff."

"And now," added Lady Clarisse, her gray eyes gleaming maliciously, "she haunts the castle, seeking her revenge."

"I see," replied Faith calmly and, as the others watched, she picked up her fork and resumed eating.

"Doesn't the story frighten you?" asked his lordship curiously.

Faith raised her eyes to his dark probing ones. "*If* I believed in ghosts, which I do not, I should judge that the people to be most fearful of it would be those resembling her husband and who thus might be mistaken for him – or beautiful women who might be mistaken for the objects of that husband's

46

affections. Since I fit neither category, I find little cause for alarm."

"Bravo, Miss Duncan," cried Mr. Felix from her side, and Faith felt a flush of pleasure. Perhaps she *was* going to get along passably well in this world that included men.

Lady Clarisse shuddered faintly and clutched the Earl's arm, but that gentleman only laughed. "I caution you, Miss Duncan, should you at any time see a figure in white flitting about the corridors, do not follow her into the shadows."

"Why not?" asked Faith practically.

The Earl smiled cynically. "There is more to the story. They say that the castle has secret passageways built into it and once an Earl, who looked like our revered ancestor, followed the apparition into the shadows and was never seen again. Speculation has it that his bones lie somewhere in a passageway where she left him dead."

"That," said Faith evenly, "is only speculation. Perhaps the gentleman in question desired to leave his position of responsibility here. What better way than to vanish without a trace? And without the annoyance of being pursued."

His lordship's dark eyes raked her as though trying to discern if she really meant what she was saying. Faith met

47

those eyes bravely. She would not bow before his arrogance. Nor would she melt all over him like butter, she thought with distaste, as Lady Clarisse seemed so fond of doing.

"I suppose you may be right," acceded his lordship. "Nevertheless, do not be foolhardy."

His eyes lingered so long on her face that she felt herself coloring up and she blurted out, "I am a very practical person, milord."

"Good. You have been forewarned and there is little more we can do. It would perhaps have been best if Felix had given you this information in London where you could have backed off."

Faith shook her head. "I should have taken the position anyway. I am not afraid of ghosts."

"Capital!" said Mr. Felix. "I knew I had made an excellent choice."

His brother shot him a quizzical look. "Yes, brother dear, inexplicable as it may seem, I believe you have."

The two men exchanged glances and Faith wondered again what could cause two brothers to so dislike each other. True, now they were exponents of diametrically opposed life-styles. But once they had been babies, children playing together. What could have destroyed the bonds of those childhood years and left them two suspicious strangers?

But that was not a question she was likely to have answered and so she addressed herself instead to an excellent apple tart.

She was preparing to rise and return to the Countess when Mr. Felix spoke. "Perhaps you would like to take a stroll outside. The fresh air would be good for you."

Faith was about to demur when his lordship chuckled harshly. "Come, we will make a party to visit the infamous cliffs." His eyes met and held hers. "Unless Miss Duncan is afraid."

Faith felt herself bristling up. "Of course I am not afraid. I was merely thinking of the Countess."

".She will be fine," his lordship assured her. "She has Deevers to sit with her and we shall not be that late."

"Very well then," agreed Faith. "I will just get my cloak and tell her ladyship that I am going."

"Of course."

As she hurried up the stairs Faith found herself wondering again why his lordship should so enjoy tormenting her. But perhaps it was part of the way in which the *ton* was accustomed to living.

Cloak in hand, she stuck her head in the

Countess's room. "We are to take a stroll outside," she said. "If your ladyship doesn't mind."

The Countess's voice carried crisply across the room. "And who might *we* be?"

"Mr. Felix and his lordship and Lady Clarisse," replied Faith, wondering at the rising tide of color she felt.

From the bed came a soft chuckle. "Very well. But do not stay out alone with Felix."

"Yes, milady. They said we shouldn't be gone long."

"Take your time. I have Deevers here."

"Thank you, milady."

Hurrying back down the stairs, Faith was puzzled. Why had the Countess warned her against staying out alone with Mr. Felix? Certainly that well-mannered man was no danger to her. It was the other one – with his dark, brooding eyes and that hard mouth that could give such savage kisses – he was the one to beware of.

Chapter 4

At the bottom of the stairs Faith found only his lordship waiting. She found, inexplicably, that her heart had risen into her throat.

"The others have not yet returned," he said, his eyes surveying her in that laconic way of his.

"I see." Faith wanted to avoid his eyes but did not know how to do it.

"I have waited here for a reason," he said, lowering his tone. "Do not stray off alone with Felix. Keep close by me."

Faith stared at him in amazement. Whatever could he mean by such a warning? She was about to ask him to explain when he raked her over with another look. "I collect that your previous employers favored drabness. Have you no gowns that do not give the impression of having been dragged through mud?"

Faith found her temper rising. How insulting he could be! "I am exceedingly sorry, milord, if my gowns offend you," she began icily.

"They do indeed," he interrupted, his eyes mocking her. "But I suppose I cannot justly

51

hold you to blame for it. It appears to me that your previous employers were rather niggardly."

Since she could not in good conscience deny this, she was forced to keep silent.

"I should take it as a great favor to me if you would make yourself some new gowns. I'll send to London for some material, something a little more amenable to the eyes."

"Your lordship is most kind," replied Faith stiffly. "But I cannot accept . . ."

His lordship's eyes caught and held hers. "There is no question of acceptance here. As my brother has no doubt told you, my aunt is very much under my influence. If I ask her to, she will make it a condition of your employment that you dress in more cheerful colors."

Faith knew when she was defeated. "Very well, milord. As you wish."

The Earl's dark eyes glittered. "That is quite often the case," he replied. "As you will soon learn, everything here is as I wish it."

Faith was about to retort to this when she heard the sound of someone approaching. Lady Clarisse and Mr. Felix could be seen coming down the hall.

"Here." His lordship took the cloak from her hand and placed it around her shoulders. As he adjusted it under the coil of her hair there was the fleeting touch of his fingers on the nape of her neck, and a strange sensation raced down her spine.

"Come," he continued. "We had best put up the hood. Even our August nights are damp."

Faith found herself standing still while his lordship tied the strings of her cloak and adjusted the hood. As his fingers left the hood, she felt the faintest caress on her cheek. Again that strange sensation traveled along her spine.

The Earl turned to his brother. "Miss Duncan and I are ready, Felix."

A strange look passed over Mr. Felix's face and was instantly gone. "Yes, indeed. And here is Lady Clarisse."

"Thank you, brother," replied the Earl.

Lady Clarisse, Faith saw, wore a cloak of light material, the hood of which formed a natural backdrop for the impressive beauty of her sable hair. She slipped an arm possessively through his lordship's. "Let's go. I have never been to the cliffs after dark. How very frightening it is." And she shivered and pressed herself closer to the Earl in a way that Faith could only regard as indelicate.

Mr. Felix drew her arm gently through his own. "The moon is some way from full, yet we should be able to see tolerably well."

His lordship nodded and moved off toward the door. His brother followed.

As the great door closed behind them, Faith breathed deeply. The night air carried only a slight chill, but there was a strange earthy smell to it. Faith sniffed again.

"You smell the moors," explained Mr. Felix. "The wind is from that direction now."

"I like it," Faith said. "It carries the smell of life."

Ahead of them his lordship snorted. "You should smell it when something dead is rotting in a bog."

"Ugh! Hugh, how very gross."

Hugh, thought Faith, she always calls him Hugh.

"Be careful here," advised Mr. Kingston solicitously. "The path is rather rocky."

"Thank you," replied Faith. Ahead of them she could see Lady Clarisse, clinging to his lordship's arm, and a strange sort of anger came over her. Some women had everything – beauty and money and a good name – and the attentions of men like the Earl.

The import of this thought having reached her consciousness, Faith suddenly stumbled. What business had she to be thinking such thoughts about an Earl, a man whose own aunt had warned her to shun him?

It was just the effect of his charm, she told herself sternly. She had had little experience of men and so was less impervious to their wiles than most women. But now that she had had some dealings with his lordship – well, she would be more careful.

The Earl turned and extended her a helping hand. Faith hesitated only momentarily. It would be rude to refuse his help under these circumstances. She placed her hand in his and was drawn up the path to stand beside him. Momentarily she felt his arm around her waist, but before she could remonstrate with him, the arm was gone and Mr. Felix had reached a place beside her.

"The cliffs are a short distance ahead," observed his lordship. "The way is somewhat treacherous."

"You will frighten Miss Duncan," said Mr. Felix, sending her a solicitous smile.

"I do not judge that Miss Duncan frightens easily," observed his lordship dryly. "Nor do I think her foolish enough to ignore warnings that are meant for her own protection."

There was more to this statement than its surface sentiment and Faith was reminded that she had received two warnings that very evening. The Countess, as well as his lordship, had warned her about going off alone with Mr. Felix. Why they should do that she could not understand, but she trusted the Countess, although she could not say the same for his lordship.

"Stop here," said his lordship, his strong arm barring the way.

Faith stopped obediently.

"We cannot see the rocks from here," complained Lady Clarisse petulantly.

"You may see the rocks in the daylight," his lordship said gruffly. "The moonlight is deceptive. I would not have any of us get too close. One misstep may propel one over the edge and in that case the view of the rocks may be closer than one expects."

"Oh, Hugh," trilled Lady Clarisse. "You are such a wit."

And you, thought Faith with an acerbity that quite astonished her, *are extremely transparent.*

And then, looking out over the moor, she quite forgot her companions. Such great beauty; Faith was awestruck. It was like an ocean, its green undulating waves capped with the pink-topped foam of heather.

Instinctively she took a step toward it and found her elbow in a tight grip. "No further, Miss Duncan," said his lordship.

"Yes, yes," faltered Faith. She turned dazzled eyes to him. "The moor – it seemed to be calling me."

The Earl's eyes were gentle and kind, entirely unlike his usual gaze. "The moor has that effect on occasion. It was this that I feared."

"I – thank you, milord."

"No thanks are necessary. I did not wish for Aunt to lose her new companion so soon."

Faith cast his lordship a glance, but he was not smiling and his tone had been entirely serious.

"Oh, Hugh, do put your arm around me. The wind is so chill," cried Lady Clarisse.

Something flickered in his lordship's eyes as they looked into Faith's. Could it be amusement? And then he put his arm around Lady Clarisse's dramatically shivering shoulders. Certainly, Faith told herself, his lordship could see through that little ploy.

For some strange reason this realization was very pleasing to her. Though why she should be pleased by the thoughts or actions of a man who meant nothing to her she could not tell.

His grip on her elbow, although it eased, did not loosen and she made no effort to escape it. Somehow with his hand holding her like that, she felt a sense of safety.

"They say that she climbed up here, hoping to escape him, but he followed her and in his rage he pushed her over."

"Perhaps it was an accident," said Faith.

"If he was drunk and she was very frightened . . ."

His lordship laughed, that harsh laugh which so unsettled her. "That was precisely the story the Earl told."

Faith turned her eyes to his. "And did they believe him?"

His lordship's eyes gleamed strangely in the moonlight. "That is impossible to say. His reputation as a pursuer of women was widely known. But so was his passion for his wife. At any rate, they did not see fit to convict him."

"He was a powerful man," added Felix. "With many friends in high places."

"And what happened to him after that?" asked Faith.

"No one knows exactly," replied his lordship. "Oh, he remarried and had a son. And then he went to sea again and never returned."

Faith found herself shivering. The story was frightening even if one didn't believe in ghosts. Love and passion were unknowns to her, too. She felt the Earl's hand slide from her elbow to enfold her fingers. In the darkness between them he squeezed her hand. Faith found the gesture strangely comforting.

"What lies there – farther east of the castle?" she asked.

"More moors," replied his lordship.

"I shall show them to you some day soon," offered Felix, and Faith was aware of a sudden spasm in his lordship's hand, the hand that in the darkness still held hers. He did not want her to walk on the moor with his brother. But why?

Faith felt entirely confused. Mr. Felix suspected his brother of wishing to hasten the old lady's death. Yet the Countess herself seemed to have some doubts about Mr. Felix. And so did his brother. And why should the Earl do something so terrible in order to gain what would eventually become his anyway? It was all too much for her, quite too much.

"Shall we return to the castle now?" asked Mr. Felix. "Or do you wish some more air?"

"It is quite lovely here," replied Faith, uneasily aware that she did not wish to leave this spot, that standing here in the darkness with her hand resting unobtrusively in the hand of his lordship, she was feeling a sort of contentment.

"I am cold," complained Lady Clarisse, moving still closer to the Earl.

"Here, Felix," he said. "Since you and Lady Clarisse are ready to go in, you go on ahead. Miss Duncan and I will enjoy the air a few moments longer and then follow you."

Faith had opened her mouth to insist that she, too, was ready to descend, when the increased pressure on her fingers stopped her. His lordship evidently wanted a word with her in private.

Mr. Kingston appeared a bit flustered by this turn of events and even in the moonlight Faith was aware of the look of smoldering hatred that was directed at her by Lady Clarisse. But the Earl cut off whatever protest the lady might have made by handing her to his brother. "Go along now. Miss Duncan and I will enjoy the air a few moments longer."

It was rather amazing, Faith thought, how his lordship got his way. For, though it was patently obvious that neither of them really wished to do so, his brother and Lady Clarisse moved off down the path.

The Earl chuckled softly. "As I said," he observed for her ears alone. "Here, things proceed as I wish them to."

Suddenly embarrassed, Faith realized that she was alone in the night with a rake. She pulled her hand loose and turned to follow the others, but the Earl was too quick for her. "Not so fast there," he said, his hand recapturing the fingers that had escaped his.

"I – it is improper to remain here," Faith faltered.

The Earl laughed. "You did not think so a moment ago." He pulled her closer so that his face was only inches from her own.

Faith found that her heart was pounding in her throat. "I – I was not thinking."

The Earl grinned wickedly. "Does my presence so endanger your senses that you cannot think?"

Faith tried to rally her wits. "It – it was not you. It was the beauty of the moors – their grandeur – that held me spellbound."

"I understand." His dark eyes mocked her. "Why then are you not looking at the moors now?"

Faith tried to wrench her eyes away from his, but could not. In fascinated horror she watched as he bent his head and his lips came closer and closer. Although she knew she should, she was unable to move away.

And then his lips covered hers and this kiss was very different from that first. This was tender, persuasive; it coaxed her very soul from her and left her weak and helpless in his arms.

The Earl buried his face in her throat. "I want you," he whispered. "And you know it. Come, I will triple what Felix pays you."

For one long moment Faith stood suspended in time. And then she spoke through stiff lips. "Kindly unhand me, milord. You quite mistake yourself. The only wages your brother pays me are for acting as nurse-companion to your aunt."

The Earl laughed, his lips moving against her throat. "Enough play-acting, my sweet. You are very good. But we are wasting precious time."

"Milord," said Faith, bringing all the scorn and acid that she could to her voice. "Did you not tell me that you never forced a woman?"

He raised his head in surprise. "Of course. I have no need of force."

"Then release me," she demanded. "I do not wish to carry this any further."

The Earl drew back in surprise. "I do not understand. I have never held a more willing woman in my arms."

"I was willing for your kiss, milord. I admit that, much as it pains me to do so. But I am not willing for anything more. I do not know why you persist in insulting me – and your brother – by imagining that I am something I am not. But whatever your deceived imagination believes that I am, you are wrong. I have spent all my grown years as nurse-companion to elderly women. The kiss that you stole from me yesterday was my first. I am truly pained to think that in my ignorance and innocence I have led you to believe unworthy things of me."

His lordship's eyes reflected first anger, then disbelief, then anger again. "If you insist, we will continue this senseless charade. Come, you will need my arm to descend."

He laughed harshly at the look of dismay on her face. "Rest assured that I shall not take advantage of you. What I told you is true. I have stolen kisses, but I have never forced a woman. Nor do I ever intend to."

There was nothing to do but put her hand in his. She could not possibly make the descent alone and unattended. She felt herself trembling at his nearness every step of the way, and as soon as they reached the great hall of the castle she mumbled her thanks and fled up the great stone stairs.

The memory of that kiss still lingered on her lips and nothing she could do seemed to erase it. But she *would* forget, she assured herself as she hurried toward the Countess's room, she *would* forget both those kisses; and any partiality that her ignorant heart might have already conceived for his lordship would be eradicated immediately. Any other course was far too dangerous even to contemplate.

Chapter 5

The days passed as days are wont to do and Faith grew more accustomed to her new surroundings. She came to know quite well that part of the castle that was not closed off.

Sometimes, when the Countess dozed and Faith stitched on the new nightdresses and chemises, she let her imagination return to the story of that Earl's ill-fated wife. How did such stories begin, she wondered? She certainly did not believe in ghosts, though sometimes she had to admit to an uncanny feeling of being watched. And she did not spend any more time than necessary in the dark shadowed halls.

It was ridiculous, of course. Even if there had been secret passageways in this castle, no one knew their location now. No, the feeling was merely the effect of an imagination overheated by his lordship's wild tales of passion and revenge. And so Faith continued stitching, repeatedly assuring herself that there were no such things as ghosts, not at all.

Once, when the Countess awoke and saw

her staring into space, she asked, "What are you thinking about, girl?"

Faith smiled. "The other night at dinner – the night we took the walk – his lordship was telling me about the ghost."

The Countess snorted. "The boy always did like to scare people. Don't pay him any mind."

"But *is* there a ghost?" asked Faith.

Against her pillows the little Countess shrugged. "Who's to say?"

"But have *you* ever heard her?" Faith's curiosity was growing.

The Countess smiled, the smile of a child contemplating mischief. "I have heard many weird sounds in this castle," she said. "But I have never *seen* a ghost."

"Oh." Faith became aware that she had clenched her hands into fists.

"I never bother myself about such things," said the old woman. "No respectable ghost would bother a sick old lady."

"And *are* there secret passageways?"

The Countess's eyes sparkled. "That boy is always up to his tricks. Life was never dull when Hugh was around. He used to spend his summers with us. It always worried me when he disappeared into the heather. But not Henry. Henry always said, 'Let the boy go. It's time he was free of his leading strings!'

65

He was like a son to my Henry. People often mistook them for father and son, those who didn't know."

"You mean –"

The Countess chuckled. "My Henry looked very like Hugh. Which is, I suppose, one of the reasons the rascal gets away with so much."

"But were you never frightened? Knowing the story and with a husband who looked like the Earl?"

The Countess shook her head. "The ghost had not bothered anyone for some years. It's not till just lately that there's been much talk of her."

"Has someone seen her?"

The Countess snorted. "You know how servants are . . ." Her warm smile seemed to exempt Faith. "And those girls Felix brought out. They were such a superstitious lot. There was some talk of this woman in white who vanished into the walls and the like. But there's been no real proof. And *I* never saw her."

"And do you think there are passageways, secret tunnels from place to place in the castle?"

The Countess wrinkled her nose. "I've never seen them myself. My Henry, though, he said he knew. Claimed he could tell me.

But I didn't want to hear. Such things are better left undisturbed. That's my feeling." Her eyes sparkled mischievously. "If the bones of dead men are lying behind these walls, I for one would just as soon *not* know it."

Faith shivered. That was a sentiment with which she was in full accord.

In an effort to change the subject, she held up her chemise. "Look, this one is almost finished. It was so kind of you to . . ."

"Stop that this instant," commanded the Countess. "I told you – the stuff was just rotting away. I hate waste."

"Yes, milady."

"By the way." The Countess's bright eyes watched Faith closely. "Hugh tells me he wants to order some dress material for you."

Faith found herself coloring up. "I told him that the gowns I have are all quite serviceable."

"And he informed *me*," replied the Countess with a wry chuckle, "that your gowns were an offense to his eyes."

"The Earl is rather top-lofty," observed Faith and then gasped. She, who had always kept her thoughts to herself, had formed the most disconcerting habit of blurting them out at the most unexpected moments.

The Countess merely chuckled. "Of course

he's top-lofty. He's been the best catch of the year for many seasons now. There are always some dowager mamas foolish enough to think that he *can* be captured. It is actually rather pathetic. Like the chicken setting out to trap the hawk. Naturally, Hugh is superior to all their schemes."

"Of course."

The Countess did not seem to hear the sarcasm in Faith's voice. "So like my Henry," the Countess continued. "Just as charming – and as arrogant."

Faith contented herself with nodding her head in agreement. If his lordship was charming, it was with a rude and arrogant charm. Of that she was certain.

Her cheeks still burned at the thought of his words on the cliff that night. How could he possibly believe that she was one of those unspeakable women? Was it lightskirts, they were called? Women who sold their favors. The very thought revolted her.

Well, she had put him properly in his place. Since that night he had hardly addressed two consecutive words to her. If he saw her in the corridors, he bowed gravely and passed on. At the dinner table he was unfailingly polite – and distant. His eyes, if they happened to light on her, were cold and empty.

It was unfortunate that the man had to go

to such extremes. But she supposed she had wounded his pride. Men were strange about things like that.

"Show me one of the nightdresses," ordered the Countess. "Hold it up so I can see if it's going to fit."

Obediently Faith draped the nightdress across the front of her gown.

There was a light tap on the door and it opened to admit his lordship. His eyes took in the nightdress and Faith's confusion and he grinned wickedly. "Very good. I see that you have taken my advice and are making a gown more pleasing to the eye."

Faith, her cheeks flooding scarlet, could find no words to answer him.

"Hugh! Now you stop badgering poor Faith. She's had little experience with men like you. What are you doing here anyway, moping around in a dreary castle while the sun is shining on the heather?"

"I was about to take myself a gallop. But first I wanted to see how you were faring."

"I'm doing quite well, m'boy. Faith here is the best medicine yet."

Faith, who had just begun to regain her normal color, flushed again. "Milady."

"Well, it's true. Say, Hugh. She's beginning to look a little peaked. Not enough sun. Take her with you."

"Oh no, I can't. That is, I have so much sewing – and your ladyship needs me."

"Nonsense. I'll call Deevers to come sit with me. We like to talk about when we were young and could wrap rascals like Hugh here around our little fingers."

"But – but –"

His lordship pulled the bell for Deevers. "You may as well give in," he said cheerfully. "Aunt is nearly as stubborn as I am. There is no withstanding the both of us."

"I – I have no riding habit. I –"

The Earl nodded. "Yes, of course, as nurse-companion to elderly ladies, you had no need of one."

His tone was above reproach, and there was no irony on the rest of his face, but his eyes told her plainly that he did not believe a word she had said.

The Countess considered for a moment. "Well, it doesn't matter. Just wear a cloak."

"I – I know very little of horses."

The Earl chuckled. "Come, you cannot escape us like that. When Aunt intends you to have fresh air, you shall have it. I will forgo my gallop and we will walk instead."

"I don't wish to interfere . . ."

"My God, girl!" snapped the Countess. "Enough talking! Get your cloak – the one with the hood – and go!"

70

"Yes, milady." The habit of years was too strong for Faith. When she was addressed in that tone, she automatically obeyed.

She hurried to her room and as quickly returned, the cloak in hand.

"And don't bring her back till she has some color in her cheeks."

The Earl gazed intently at Faith until he saw her color rising and then he laughed. "Be assured, Aunt, I will see that she gets plenty of air."

And before Faith quite knew how it had happened, his fingers were on her elbow, propelling her out the door and down the stairs.

The Earl was silent as they moved across the great hall, and Faith was still somewhat stunned. The last thing in her mind had been to put herself in such a position with his lordship. But there was no stopping the Countess when she wished to have her way. In that she was very like her nephew.

If Spacks thought it odd that they should be leaving the castle together, his face did not reveal it. His features were set in a perpetual expression of despair that Faith had come to realize was normal for him.

As the great door closed behind them, his lordship paused. "You have forgotten to put on your cloak. Let me help you."

71

Before she could reply he had taken the cloak from her hands and put it around her shoulders. Again his fingers moved deftly under the coil of her hair, brushing the nape of her neck and causing the strangest sensations to race down her spine.

Then he tucked her arm through his and set off. At first the path led between some carefully nurtured trees. "The soil here is not the best for trees, but we do what we can. The birch and pine manage to carry on."

Faith was afraid to speak, afraid to even look at him. Why had his aunt insisted on such a walk? She could acquire fresh air by herself by stepping out into the courtyard, although admittedly she had not. She had, after all, been busy. What with attending to the Countess and stitching on her clothes, her time had been full.

"I shall send to London tomorrow for some material," announced his lordship suddenly.

Faith started. It was almost as though this man could read her mind. "You are very kind," she said demurely.

The Earl stopped in midstride. "I believe you are mocking me," he said, his eyes gleaming with dark humor. "It is not a matter of kindness at all. Rather, it is a case of pure selfishness. Since I am the one offended by your gowns, it stands to reason that I should pay for changing them. Does it not?"

Faith found the whole question embarrassing and she felt her cheeks turn scarlet as she spoke. "I do not know much about such matters, but it appears to me that for a gentleman to provide me with the stuff for dresses is improper."

"Of course." His voice grated harshly. "I keep forgetting about your innocence." His eyes gleamed down into hers and she saw he still did not believe her.

She determined to ignore this. Since she was compelled to walk with him there was little profit in being at sword point during the whole jaunt. "Her ladyship has told me that I am to make some new dresses and I shall do so," she said evenly. "So there is little cause for further discussion."

"Good." He looked around him. "Have you ever been in country like this before?"

Faith shook her head. "No, my life has been spent in London. I know little of the countryside."

The Earl's dark features hardened. "The moors are beautiful, especially when the heather is in bloom, as now. But they are dangerous too." He looked at her. "They are rather like a certain kind of woman – beautiful on the outside and rotten underneath."

73

"I do not understand," said Faith.

"The soil of the moors can support only certain types of growth like heather, sedges, and some grasses. And these rolling stretches of land have their own innate beauty. But in other places this beauty hides boggy areas – dangerous places for man or beast. Or woman. Someone who has fallen into a bog may vanish without a trace."

Faith's heart pounded. Could he be threatening her? She could not tell.

"Are the moors good for anything?" she asked hesitantly, in an effort to calm her ridiculous fears.

His lordship looked out over the distance. "Many people graze sheep on them. We have not kept sheep for some time now."

"I see."

They had now moved some distance from the castle. His lordship stooped, picked a sprig of heather, and gravely tucked it into her hair.

"Thank you," murmured Faith. "Your aunt tells me that you know the moors well."

The Earl smiled. "They were my childhood home. Every year I longed for the summer months that I could spend free and wild on the heath."

"You must know the area very well then," Faith said.

74

His lordship nodded. "Very well. Come, I will show you something." And he set out again.

For some moments Faith had no breath to spare for conversation as his lordship moved on with great strides. She felt the ground under her thin house shoes changing texture as he hurried her up and down the heathered slopes.

Finally he stopped. "Do you see anything different here?"

Faith shook her head. "No."

The Earl laughed. "Two more steps would have you mired in the bog. So mired, in fact, that you might never escape. There are low spots in the bog. You might be walking ankle deep and all of a sudden be in it to your waist." His glance slid over her slowly.

Faith shuddered. "How can you tell?"

"I know this place so well that I can sense it from the feel of the sod beneath my boots." He smiled, a strangely enigmatic smile. "Look around you. Where is the castle from here?"

Faith turned. "Why it's right be –" She stared in astonishment at the vast, rolling expanse of infertile land, empty land, that seemed to stretch in all directions. "I don't understand."

"The lay of the land is deceptive. The

hills are small, but their rolling effect is confusing."

"Where *is* the castle?" asked Faith, increasingly and nervously aware that she was alone on the heath with this dark brooding man.

The Earl's eyes searched hers. "This is dangerous country," he repeated. "Do not ever venture out here alone." His eyes seemed to be searching hers for something. "Nor should you ever come with Felix – or Clarisse, for that matter."

"You are certainly a suspicious sort of person," Faith found herself retorting. She could see that Lady Clarisse might feel like pushing her into a bog, especially if she knew what had passed between Faith and his lordship. But Mr. Felix – poor, kind man – how could his brother suspect him of such awful things?

The Earl took her hands in his. "You must promise me this," he urged.

Faith struggled to release her hands. It was strangely disconcerting to be held so, with those black eyes peering into her own.

"Promise me," he repeated.

"All right," Faith replied. "I think it is a silly promise, but I will make it. But I do not see why either of them should ask me here."

The Earl smiled. "You do the innocent capitally. The stage lost a great actress when you entered your present profession."

Faith felt her cheeks turning red. There he went again, accusing her of being one of those infamous women. "Milord!"

"Yes, yes, I know. I am utterly mistaken. No matter. For now we are not Earl and nurse-companion. That is all forgotten. We will be merely man and woman, enjoying a walk together on the moor. Agreed?"

Faith hesitated. "I – I do not know."

The Earl laughed. "You have never been on a walk with a man?"

The color flooded her face again. "Only the other night when we went to the cliffs."

The Earl shook his head and his eyes took on that unbelieving look.

"I am sorry to offend you with the facts of my previous existence, milord," she said stiffly. "But facts are facts." For some strange reason she felt foolish tears rising to her eyes and hastily took a step away from him.

Suddenly the earth seemed to give beneath her feet. "Oh!" Faith's arms flailed out in panic and a scream rose to her throat.

The next instant the Earl had reached out and pulled her from danger. She came to rest against a striped waistcoat and was held there by a pair of strong arms. Her heart pounded in her throat, but as her thoughts began to focus again, she could not tell if its wild beating was caused by the nearly averted danger or by the terrible breath-stopping nearness of the man whose arms held her captive. For a long moment she felt suspended in time and then sanity returned.

"Milord," she stammered. "You must release me."

"Look at me," he commanded harshly, as though he had not heard her at all.

Hesitantly Faith raised her head. "Milord," she repeated.

He was glaring at her. "Little fool! I had just warned you of the danger and you walk right into it."

Faith felt herself caught by those dark, probing eyes. They seemed to be searching her own, searching for something unknown to her. "I – You were angry with me," she blurted out. "I didn't think."

"Surely your previous employers were not always even tempered." His eyes mocked her.

Faith shook her head. "Of course not. Some of them were rather sharp-tongued."

"Then why should a few cutting words from me cause you to lose all discretion?"

"I – You are a man and . . ." She knew she should stop. She knew these were not proper words for a young woman to utter, but he seemed to be drawing her thoughts out of her. "And you frighten me."

"I?" His lordship's eyebrows rose quizzically. "Frighten you?"

Faith nodded. "I am unused to the ways of men and you are – are –"

"Say it," he commanded harshly.

"You – are a rake."

For a moment his dark eyes regarded her cynically and then he laughed. "I must admit that you are amusingly good in your part."

Faith felt herself bristling up. Why did the man never believe her? "I'll thank you to unhand me," she said with as much dignity as she could muster. "I see no reason why I must bear your repeated insults."

"Indeed." His dark eyes laughed at her. "You are in the midst of the moor surrounded by dangerous bog and your only companion – and the only one who can lead you to safety – is a declared rake. It appears to me that you will have to bear whatever insults I choose to deliver."

"I – Please let me go." She struggled against the force of his arms, but he merely laughed. "If I release you, you will only go floundering off into the bog and probably end up soaked. I prefer not to have to wet my boots."

"You – you are quite beyond the line," Faith cried.

"Indeed." His lordship's eyes danced. "That is certainly a cavalier attitude to take toward one who had just saved your life."

"Saved my life!" Faith sputtered angrily.

The Earl's face darkened. "Undeniably. If I chose to leave you here, it is extremely doubtful that you could find your way back to the castle, is it not?"

Faith was forced to nod. But even worse was the growing realization that some incorrigibly insane part of her did not really wish to be released from his lordship's arms. They held for her a strange sense of security. Confused by the recognition of feelings that she was sure no respectable young woman should ever have, she dropped her eyes again. "I think it's time to go back. Her ladyship . . ."

"Her ladyship will be chatting away with Deevers. Her instructions were for you to get some fresh air."

"But I have," Faith murmured, still afraid to raise her eyes.

"I am the judge of that," averred his lordship. His gloved hand reached under her chin and tilted her head back until her eyes met his. Then critically he searched her face.

"Your cheeks are not yet of a sufficiently rosy hue."

His eyes met hers and Faith felt that strange sensation along her spine. What power the man had! And then, as she watched unable to move, he bent his head and took her lips.

There was savagery in this kiss, she thought, as though he wished to ravage her very soul. But there was also that devastating tenderness. And then the waves of feeling swept over her and all thought vanished.

Some moments later his lordship raised his head. Gradually Faith forced herself back to reality. "Milord, I thought you never forced a woman." She made her tone as acid as she could.

His eyes were filled with mockery. "That's right, I do not."

"But just now —"

His lips trailed along her throat in a way that left her quite weak. "There was no force here. You forget, my pet, that I am a man of experience. When I looked into your eyes, I clearly read your desire to be kissed. And I obliged."

Faith stiffened in his arms. "You are quite abominable. Release me this instant."

The Earl laughed. "You may deny it all you please. My senses do not lie to me. Not now. Not before. And now —" He kissed the tip of her nose lightly. "Now we shall continue our exercise. I am a patient man and I shall wait until you are ready for me."

And with that the Earl removed his arms, took her by the hand, and led her carefully away from the swampy ground.

Chapter 6

The sun was no longer high in the sky when Faith and his lordship returned to the castle. By this time no one could deny the bloom in her cheeks or a certain bright sparkle in her eyes that even Faith herself was unaware of.

As they entered the great door she could not help observing the disapproving look that Spacks bestowed on them. But she would not worry about it, she told herself. Because of her position she was not within the butler's jurisdiction and, because she dined with Mr. Felix and the others, and not at the first table with the upper servants, she did not have to deal with Spacks.

"I must return to the Countess," said Faith, aware that she would much prefer to stay with his lordship.

"Ah, but you shall not return alone." His

lordship's eyes sparkled with mischief. "I intend to deliver you safely to her very door and receive my due praise for your rosy cheeks. Your beauty, unfortunately, I can take no credit for. I would if I could, believe me."

Faith's cheeks grew even rosier. She was not beautiful and she said so. "You are kind, milord, but you forget. I have a cheval glass of my own and I do not see beauty in it."

His lordship shrugged as they moved on up the stairs. "Your eyes are dimmed by too many years in maiden establishments. It is time you faced reality." He grinned wickedly at her. "You forget that I am a man most qualified to make such a judgment. Have I not, as a great rake and pursuer of womankind, been equally pursued by all the *ton's* most eminent beauties? Believe me, I know whereof I speak."

By this time they had reached the door of the Countess's room and Faith was spared a reply. The Earl knocked once and entered.

From her place beside the great bed Deevers turned curious eyes on them and, to Faith's amazement, beamed on his lordship. "Ah, there you are, milord. You're looking so handsome, you are."

His lordship pulled Faith closer to the bed. "And you, Deevers, are getting to be an old flatterer. Just because you dandled me on your knee does not mean I grew up to be handsome."

Deevers continued to beam as she left the room, and from her nest of pillows the Countess chuckled. "You scamp, you. You know perfectly well what a devilish handsome man you are. You don't need two old ladies to tell you so."

His lordship laughed. "You have me again, Aunt. But you see," his eyes moved over Faith and back to his aunt, "I have been endeavoring to muster a suitable modesty in order to impress Miss Duncan, who believes, I fear, that I am incurably top-lofty."

Faith gasped but the Countess merely chuckled. "My dear Hugh, such modesty would be false indeed. If ever a man knew his own worth, that man is you."

His lordship bowed. "If you are not careful, Aunt, you will turn my head."

This time the Countess laughed outright. "Hugh, my boy, I am far too late for that." She turned critical eyes on Faith. "I see by your cheeks that your walk was a bracing one."

"Yes, milady." Faith did not know how else to reply, conscious of his lordship's mocking eyes upon her.

And then he spoke. "I think the fresh air

was most invigorating for her. Do you note the sparkle in her eyes?"

Faith was covered in confusion. "Milord," she protested, but he continued to regard her and, as the Countess too turned bright eyes upon her, she wanted to run away.

"Indeed, Hugh, it must have been *very* invigorating. I hope you were not up to your old tricks."

"I?" His lordship's dark handsome features took on an expression of such aggrieved innocence that Faith felt an insane desire to giggle. "Dear Aunt, a man of the world does not need tricks." His eyes touched Faith's mockingly and moved back to his aunt. "And besides, I'm certain you know by now the story of Miss Duncan's life. Surely you would not suspect me of leading an innocent astray?"

Faith, hearing the undercurrent of sarcasm, wanted to scream at him that she *was* innocent and that she could not help it, but she forced herself to remain silent. He had not believed her before and he would not believe her now. Why should he?

The Countess eyed her shrewdly. "Go along now, Hugh. You have harassed and invigorated the girl enough. The outing has achieved its purpose."

His lordship approached the bed and kissed his aunt tenderly on the cheek. "If I promise not to harass her, you will send her down to dinner, won't you? Dining with Felix and Clarisse is enough to make a man unsocial."

The Countess laughed again and touched his cheek with a withered hand. "How shamelessly you play on my affection for you," she said. "You know how like my Henry you are." She sighed wistfully.

"I cannot love you as Henry did," said his lordship in a tender tone that Faith had never before heard him employ. "But I do love you, Aunt."

There was a long moment of silence and Faith felt that she should not be witnessing a scene of such intimacy. And then the Countess broke the silence. "I know it, my boy. I know it. Now run along and leave an old lady to rest. You'll find Miss Duncan at the dinner table as usual."

"Thank you, Aunt." The gravity was gone from his voice and the look he gave Faith was one of sheer mischief. And then he was gone, striding across the room and out the door with the air of a man who commanded everything in sight.

But not me, Faith found herself thinking, and wondered why the thought should be a painful one.

"Well, Faith," said the Countess. "Do not stand there staring into space. Take off your cloak and come sit down. Tell me how you found the moors. Henry and I used to take long walks there in my salad days."

And so Faith removed her cloak and settled on a chair by the bed, determined to remember and relate to the Countess every detail of the beauty of the moor and even more determined to drive from her mind, heart, and soul the memories of the Earl's arms, the Earl's lips, the Earl's insulting words about being a patient man, a man who could wait.

She was almost through her recital of the beauties of their walk when the door opened to admit the Lady Clarisse. "Dear Aunt, I hope you are well."

The lady's eyes sped over the room. Was she looking for something? wondered Faith. Or someone?

"I am getting better every day," said the Countess. "Most particularly because of Faith here."

"Oh yes, yes. Of course."

It was plain to Faith that Lady Clarisse did not mean a word of this and, when she glanced at the Countess, Faith realized that the old lady, too, put little credence in her niece's statements.

"And what have you been doing with yourself?" the Countess asked.

Lady Clarisse shrugged. "The usual things,

a little reading, a little needlepoint. And I had meant to take a walk with his lordship, but he seems to have vanished."

"He was showing Faith the moors," said the Countess bluntly.

"Oh." The monosyllable seemed to have escaped before Lady Clarisse could prevent it. "Is that – that is – do you think it wise?"

"I do not know what *it* you are referring to," replied the Countess severely. "But I told Hugh to take Faith out for some fresh air. She works very hard seeing to my comfort and it is bad for her to be cooped up all the time."

"Yes, yes, of course," repeated the Lady Clarisse. "I was only thinking – I mean, Miss Duncan's position and Hugh being what he is. You wouldn't want a scandal, I'm sure."

The Countess gave her niece a shrewd look. "There'll be no scandal in this castle, Clarisse, I assure you. Nor do I believe that Hugh would care for these aspersions on his character."

Lady Clarisse laughed awkwardly and for the first time Faith saw her back down from someone. "No, no, I meant nothing like that." She cast an appealing glance at the old woman. "I only meant to help."

"I have heard your advice and will consider

it," said the Countess in a tone so cold that it made Faith want to shiver. But Lady Clarisse seemed to have regained her aplomb and merely nodded.

"Yes, well – I won't keep you from your rest, Aunt. Good day." The lady moved gracefully to the door.

It had barely closed behind her when the Countess snorted. "That one has the soul of a banker. She never gave a piece of advice that wasn't designed to benefit herself."

"Why," Faith found herself asking, "if you feel so about her, why do you allow her here?"

"I thought about sending her packing, in spite of her mother," said the Countess with a frown. "It's plain she's after Hugh. An Earl is just what she wants. But she is my sister's girl. I loved my sister." There was a pause. "I spoke to Hugh about her, warned him, in fact. But he merely laughed. He had long ago smelled out her kind, he reminded me, and he quite knew how to deal with her. He amuses himself, nothing more. And so I let her stay on. It helps pass the time for him. And it does me no harm. Her duty calls are fortunately as brief as the one she just made. But enough of her. You had best dress for dinner."

And so, long before she was prepared to meet the Earl's eyes again, Faith was on her way down the great stone staircase. As

89

she reached the bottom she was surprised to find the Lady Clarisse waiting for her. "Miss Duncan?"

"Yes, milady."

"I – I do not quite know how to say this to you. But for your own good I feel it must be said."

"Yes, milady." Faith kept her voice as noncommittal as possible. There was little point in aggravating the woman further.

"For your own safety you must avoid being alone with his lordship. He is not fit company for an innocent young woman."

"Yes, milady." Faith refused to let her anger show. "I know."

This simple statement seemed to reassure Lady Clarisse, thought Faith with an inner smile as she moved on toward the dining room. How could such a lady of the world be taken in so easily?

But then her thoughts were removed from the Lady Clarisse by the sight of his lordship, elegantly turned out.

"Good evening, your lordship."

"Good evening, Miss Duncan," replied the Earl, his eyes moving easily over her. "I hope our walk did not fatigue you unduly."

"No, milord," replied Faith demurely, and then some imp inside her, driven perhaps by the knowledge that the Lady Clarisse was right behind her, forced her to add, "Indeed, I found it most invigorating."

His lordship's eyes sparked with mischief. "We shall do it again soon then," he replied.

"Hugh, my dear." Lady Clarisse swept into the room with a swish of silk and an aura of heavy scent.

"Lady Clarisse." The Earl turned from Faith and made his greeting to the lady. "Good evening."

"Oh, Hugh," she cooed. "Don't be so formal with me. You act as though we had just met."

"Indeed, Lady Clarisse," replied the Earl in a tone of reprimand. "*I* thought I was acting with the courtesy due a *lady*."

A curious stress on this last word was not lost on Faith's ears, but she didn't turn her head to observe Lady Clarisse's reaction. His lordship seemed to think that all women had been previously taken. Perhaps, she thought, that made his approach to them more palatable to his conscience.

And then Mr. Felix turned from the sideboard and smiled at her. "Miss Duncan, how well you look this evening."

"Thank you, sir. That is most kind of you."

"She has been for a walk on the moors," said Lady Clarisse, "with your brother."

"Indeed." Mr. Felix's smile vanished swiftly. "That was hardly wise."

Faith looked at him in surprise.

"The moors are wild and dangerous," Mr. Felix said with concern. "A stranger may easily get lost there."

Faith nodded. "I have been warned. And I will not venture out there by myself, I assure you."

"That is a good decision," Mr. Felix agreed. "If you need air, you may walk about the castle yard."

"Or up on the cliffs," said Lady Clarisse with a sweetness that sickened Faith. It did not take her previous warning from the Countess or the strange look that the Earl sent her to make Faith resolve never to go on the cliffs if the Lady Clarisse was nearby.

"It was the Countess's wish that I go for this walk," Faith said evenly. She wanted Mr. Felix to know the truth. He was, after all, not the sort of man to countenance a young woman's walking about alone with a rake. And she valued Mr. Felix's good opinion of her. It was nice to know that some man understood her, that some man recognized innocence and valued it. His believe in her helped to uphold her self-respect, a respect that his lordship's assault on her senses did nothing to increase.

As Mr. Felix drew her arm courteously through his and moved toward the dinner table, a curious look crossed his lordship's face. It was quite fleeting and the next second he was laughing at something whispered by the Lady Clarisse.

Faith felt a strange stirring of anger. What right had he to look at her like that? And even more so, to look at *her* and then to smile so winningly at that woman!

Chapter 7

And so the last days of August moved slowly by. His lordship's morning visits to his aunt continued to be a daily occurrence and Faith, to her dismay, found herself looking forward to them. This was patently foolish and she told herself so impatiently whenever her heart beat faster at his entrance.

Inevitably he would chat with his aunt and remark on whatever piece of clothing she chanced to be stitching. In self-defense Faith took to working on her chemises and nightdresses at other times. The thought of his lordship viewing these articles of her intimate apparel brought a heated glow to her cheeks.

It was perhaps a week after their excursion on the moors that he arrived carrying a large parcel. "My rider has returned from London. His mission was quite successful." He extended the parcel to her.

Faith felt her cheeks coloring and hesitated. "Milord," she faltered.

The Earl looked at the Countess. "Come, Faith," she said briskly. "I thought this was all settled. Bring it here and let me see the colors."

Obediently Faith took the package and moved toward the big bed. His lordship followed her. With trembling hands Faith untied the parcel to reveal a riotous array of colors.

"Oh!" Never in her life had she seen so many lengths of material in such glorious colors. Tears rose unbidden to her eyes. "Oh, milady."

"Well, well, Hugh, my boy," said the Countess. "You have outdone yourself this time."

His lordship chuckled. "It was nothing, Aunt. Come, help me decide which she should make first."

Faith stood by with awed eyes as the Earl held swath after swath of material up to her.

"They are all superbly suited to her coloring, Hugh. How did you achieve that?"

The Earl laughed. "Dear Aunt, you forget that I am a connoisseur of beauty. I simply sent the man to a dressmaker I know with the name of a current reigning beauty whose complexion and coloring most approximate that of Miss Duncan."

He smiled. "I believe I prefer the rose-lavender first, Aunt. What do you think?"

The Countess nodded. "That should do admirably. I am also particularly fond of this pale green. It complements her hair so well."

Faith, listening to this discussion about herself, felt embarrassment. She could not help letting her eyes rest momentarily on the Earl.

"I also asked the dressmaker to include a book of the latest patterns. I do not want to find this stuff made into outmoded gowns like those she has been wearing."

"Of course, Hugh, my boy. I'll see to it."

In spite of her great gratitude, Faith was conscious of a tiny surge of anger. How terribly overbearing the man was! Arrogant, top-lofty, high in the instep, tyrannical – she could go on and on. And yet there was a strange stirring in her heart whenever he entered the room.

"You *will* make the rose-lavender first,

95

will you not?" he asked with a smile that threatened to melt her very bones.

"Yes, milord," she murmured. "If that is your wish."

"It is," he said, and there was something strange in his voice, some tone that she could not quite recognize which made her raise her eyes to his. For the briefest moment she thought she saw tenderness there. Then it was gone, whatever she had seen, and she realized that it could not have been tenderness. Such men did not *feel* tenderness; it was foreign to their very natures.

Blindly she reached out for the material and found that her hand had been touched by another, a strong brown hand that sent tremors through her flesh. She wanted to pull her hand away, but it seemed that she could not.

The Earl turned to his aunt. "I shall take myself off for a walk on the moors."

Faith's heart leaped into her throat, but he continued smoothly. "When you have finished your first gown – the heather one – I shall take you for another walk."

And then, before she could reply, almost before she realized that the material was the exact colour of the sprig of heather which lay between the pages of her only book, he was gone.

"Come here, Faith, and look at these," said the Countess. "I want to be in on the choosing of the pattern."

"Of course, milady." Faith automatically turned back toward the bed, but her mind, for some foolish reason, kept reverting to that walk on the heather. Had he done this on purpose, she kept asking herself? Could that day have meant something to *him*, something so important that he had specifically ordered material to remind her of it?

But surely that was impossible. It was probably a coincidence, or perhaps, the thought chilled her, perhaps this was one of the evidences of his charm. Perhaps this was the way he won the beauties of London.

"Faith, you are woolgathering." The Countess broke into her thoughts.

"I'm sorry, milady. It's just – it's overwhelming. So much – I never dreamed . . ."

The Countess patted her hand reassuringly. "You are a good girl, Faith. And life has been difficult for you. Now, for the first time you have a chance to sample its good things. And without harm to yourself. Do not be afraid of Hugh. He's a good boy basically. He is being kind to you because I'm so pleased with you."

"But, milady. He is – his reputation . . ." Faith could not continue.

97

The Countess shook her head. "Hugh has done his share. Obviously he's no novice in the petticoat line. But he respects innocence. I have spoken to him privately, my dear. You need not fear him."

Faith nodded. For some reason she found that she could not tell her employer of the Earl's suspicions about her. They were unfounded, of course, but would the Countess believe that? Faith could not be sure. And so she kept silent, turning her attention to the pattern book.

"Yes, milady. Which of these do you prefer?"

"Well, I rather like this design. What do you think?"

The picture to which the Countess pointed showed a gown with a bodice gathered high and from it the skirt fell straight to the floor. That part was not too bad, but the neckline caused Faith's hand to fly to her throat in dismay. The rounded neckline dipped dangerously low in front, showing a great deal of throat and . . .

Faith's thoughts stopped there. And the sleeves – they were merely little puffs at the shoulders that left the rest of the arms bare.

"Isn't it a little bare?" asked Faith softly.

The Countess laughed. "You are excessively modest, my dear. This neckline

98

is nothing like those of my girlhood. Now those were *low*."

"Yes, milady," repeated Faith but her mind had moved into the future, a future in which she was appearing before his lordship's speculative eyes in the new gown of heather pink. In her imagination she saw those dark brooding eyes sliding over her body. Would he approve of what he saw, she wondered, a flush rising to her cheeks again.

"Yes, this is the gown, my dear," said the Countess. "You must get Deevers to help you with the cutting. And do hurry, I am anxious to see you in it."

"Yes, milady," Faith answered. "I'll start today." And, gathering the material to her breast, she hastened to her room.

The rest of the day was spent in cutting, pinning, stitching and fitting. By the time she reached the dinner table her head was awhirl.

"You are pale this evening," remarked his lordship.

"I – I have been working hard," Faith replied.

"Ah," said the Earl with a secret smile. "Stitching, no doubt."

"Stitching?" echoed Lady Clarisse with such surprise that Mr. Felix turned to look.

"Yes," said his lordship, and Faith felt

herself coloring up. If he mentioned that *he* had bought her material, Mr. Felix would hear him and suppose the worst – he must. Her heart pounded in her throat. Mr. Felix's good opinion of her was important. Lately he had been even kinder than usual, smiling on her with a genial friendliness every time he met her.

"Yes," continued his lordship with a smile. "Aunt thought that Miss Duncan needed some new gowns. And so we dispatched a man to London to fetch some stuff for them."

Carefully Faith let out her breath. He *had* had a care for her reputation. He *had* protected her name.

"I see," replied Lady Clarisse with a smile at his lordship that caused a tightening in Faith's throat. Deliberately she looked in another direction. What Lady Clarisse did with the Earl was no concern of hers. No concern at all.

Mr. Felix approached Faith with a smile. "Aunt seems very pleased with your services," he said pleasantly.

"Yes, sir," replied Faith. "She's a very pleasant person, very kindhearted."

Mr. Felix cast her a look of surprise which clearly indicated that he himself had not been the recipient of much of the Countess's kindness. For the hundredth time Faith wondered why Mr. Felix and his aunt did not deal well together. Both of them seemed to be kind, generous persons. And, Mr. Felix had gone to a great deal of trouble to get her a nurse-companion.

Well, she put such thoughts from her mind. There was no way she could resolve the problem. She simply must do her best for each of them.

By the time the meal was over – a very satisfactory meal topped off with an apple tart – Faith had forgotten about the material and was just feeling comfortably full and relaxed.

"Come, Hugh," said Lady Clarisse. "I want you to read to me – in the drawing room."

"Of course, my dear. What shall I read?"

"I have something in mind," said Lady Clarisse coyly. "I will show you."

"If you will excuse us?" said his lordship, his eyes meeting Faith's only temporarily.

"Of course," replied Mr. Felix. "Go right ahead. I have a few things to discuss with Miss Duncan."

"Yes, of course," replied the Earl. "Naturally." This time he let his eyes linger on her face, mocking her.

But Lady Clarisse soon pulled him away and Faith was left alone with Mr. Felix. She was not disturbed at being alone with him.

Such a kind man was no threat to her. Now, if it had been his lordship ... She pushed the thought from her mind. Whatever Mr. Felix wanted to discuss with her was purely a business matter.

She rose from the table and Mr. Felix was instantly at her side. "If you'll come with me, Miss Duncan, we can speak more privately in the library."

"Yes, sir," Faith replied, and smiled as he drew her arm gently through his and led her down the hall.

Inside the library he led her to a divan and gestured to her to be seated. Then he settled himself beside her. He stared intently into her eyes. "Miss Duncan, I – I have something important to say to you."

"Yes, sir?" asked Faith.

"I find this difficult to say," he went on. "I – I am not a man of the world. But you are a fine young woman. I have watched you closely. You would make some man a fine wife."

"Thank you, sir," murmured Faith, hardly believing her ears.

"I know this is too soon. I would not frighten you. But someday, someday in the not too distant future, I have a question to ask you. I wish to give you time for consideration." He pressed her hand warmly.

"That's all for tonight. I will say no more at the moment."

"Yes, please," Faith managed to stammer. It seemed impossible but Mr. Felix must be talking about – about marriage! The thought stunned her. She had thought of Mr. Felix as a kindhearted, genial man. She had never thought of him as a prospective husband. In fact, she had never considered any man as a prospective husband – except in moments of the sheerest insanity when the Earl's dark brooding face flashed before her eyes.

She rose unsteadily. "I believe I must return to your aunt, sir," she said.

Mr. Felix shook his head. "Don't you remember? Aunt send word that Deevers would be sitting with her. She wants you to have a little relaxation."

Faith nodded. "Yes, yes. I forgot."

He smiled on her genially as he again drew her arm through his and moved toward the library. In a sort of daze Faith allowed herself to be drawn along at his side.

Before the hearth in the library Lady Clarisse was stretched out on a divan in an attitude of elegance, while before her, on a low stool that caused him to look up to see her, sat his lordship. Faith privately thought the whole scene somewhat overdone. The airs that Lady Clarisse affected might be attractive to men, but in Faith's eyes they were definitely in bad taste.

Of course, Faith admitted to herself, her upbringing as a motherless girl and her subsequent life in service to eccentric old ladies had not given her much idea of the doings of high society. Although she was of good blood, Papa had disdained all the business of the *haut ton* as a bushel of tomfoolery. Consequently Faith knew very little about men of his lordship's stamp.

"Oh, Hugh!" breathed Lady Clarisse in honeyed tones, causing Faith to stifle an exclamation of disgust. "You read so beautifully. Please continue."

His lordship looked at his brother and Faith questioningly. "Yes, indeed, Hugh, do continue. You've always read well," said Felix.

The Earl smiled, that lazy insolent smile that Faith could not quite understand. "Very well. This is called 'The First Kiss of Love.' "

"I absolutely adore Byron," breathed the Lady Clarisse as Mr. Felix settled Faith and himself on a nearby divan.

Faith closed her eyes as the Earl began to read. His voice was deep and low; it held tones she had never heard in it before, tones almost like a caress, she told herself, her face heating at the thought.

"Away with your fictions of flimsy
    romance,
Those tissues of falsehood which folly
    has wove!
Give me the mild beam of the soul-
    breathing glance,
Or the rapture which dwells on the
    first kiss of love."

The rest of the words were lost on Faith, who
had returned in memory to *her* first kiss. How
savage and brutal that kiss had been. The Earl
had been a stranger to her and she to him.
Not a bit of tenderness in it and yet, she had
enjoyed it. Her face and throat grew even
more heated. But of course, she told herself
quite emphatically, that had *not* been a kiss of
love.

How could a man like the Earl know about
love? Real love? And yet the Countess had
spoken of the late Earl, her husband, as
having *loved* her. And by all accounts he was
very like his lordship in actions as well as in
looks.

Still, she must realize that the present
Earl had thought of that kiss as a sampling
of merchandise which he was considering
purchasing.

Faith became conscious that Mr. Felix was

patting her hand and then she grew aware that everyone was looking at her.

"My brother has finished the reading," said Mr. Felix. "And he has asked for your opinion on his efforts."

"Oh! I am sorry. I was thinking of something else."

The Earl smiled cynically. "I see that my reading could not have been very good. Not if I could not hold your attention." Those dark eyes fastened on hers mockingly.

"Oh no! I was remem –" Faith stopped in confusion. If she said that she was remembering her first kiss, either he would think that his opinion of her as a low woman was correct or he would think that she was recalling *his* kiss. Either possibility caused her great embarrassment.

"You are an excellent reader," she said with as much calmness as she could manage. "The timbre of your voice is very effective."

"Thank you," said his lordship dryly. "Tell me, what do you think of Byron's line. 'Man's love is to man a thing apart, 'Tis woman's whole existence'?"

Faith paused. "I have not previously heard or read Byron's work."

"Not read Byron!" cried Lady Clarisse in horror. "How dreadful."

"Miss Duncan led a sheltered existence

before she came to us," commented the Earl. "Byron is seldom found in the libraries of rich old harridans. The mere mention of men is anathema in such households. Am I not right, Miss Duncan?"

Faith felt the scarlet flood her cheeks again. Why did his lordship cause her to blush so often? "I really cannot be so rude as to speak of my previous employers as harridans," she replied evenly. "And I cannot speak for the households of all such ladies because I only served in a few. However, I can say that Lord Byron was not mentioned in any of the households where I served. I did occasionally read about him in the newspapers, but I never had the opportunity to read his poetry."

The Earl continued to wear his mocking smile and Lady Clarisse simply stared. Finally, Faith broke the silence. "Since this is the first time I have heard the lines you just read I have not had much time to consider them. I think that he is quite possibly right. However, I have very little experience of men and so I cannot judge what love is to them."

Mr. Felix smiled approvingly on such a reasonable statement, but his lordship frowned. It seemed that he would never believe her innocent.

"And what of women's feelings?" he inquired with a searching look.

Faith sighed. "The nature of my life has been such that I have known few women, so I really have little knowledge of their feelings."

"And your own?" he persisted.

"I – I do not know," Faith faltered. "Since I have never been in love I am unequipped to judge if it could be my whole existence."

His Lordship's eyes held hers captive. He seemed to be seeking something there, trying to discover something in their depths. Faith forced herself to return his gaze, but as she did so she grew aware of a strange sensation creeping over her. It was almost as though he could master her soul merely by looking at her.

She felt a little shiver. A woman's soul should belong to no one but God. And as for her existence – to build it on love of such a man as the Earl, an acknowledged rake, would surely be an act of sheer stupidity.

Finally, when she thought she could bear the steady gaze of those eyes no longer, the Earl turned back to Lady Clarisse. Greatly relieved and yet somehow disappointed, Faith got to her feet. "Please excuse me, Mr. Felix. Milord. Milady. Mrs. Deevers has other things to be about and I promised to read to the Countess."

"All right," said Mr. Felix genially. "If you

insist. But we shall be sorry to lose your company."

Lady Clarisse seemed to be trying to hide a smile of pleasure, but his lordship merely nodded. And so Faith made her way back up the dark staircase to the Countess. And as she went she pondered over the power that his lordship seemed to have over women. And – much as she would have liked to deny it – over her.

Chapter 8

More days passed, busy days for Faith, whose fingers seemed eternally stitching, stitching on the dress the color of heather blossoms. And finally it was done.

It was with no little trepidation that Faith carried the newly finished dress to her room and slipped into it. As it fell down around her she felt a growing nervousness. What sort of look would appear in the eyes of the Earl when she came down to dinner in this gown that was really *his* gift?

What did she look like, she wondered, turning to the cheval glass. And then she gasped. The soft stuff of the gown clung to her, outlining a body which she had been only vaguely aware of. Why, she thought with a quiver of anxiety, the gown was almost indecent! It not only clung to her body, but it seemed to display a dangerous amount of throat – and more. And her arms, bare as they were, seemed so white against the rose-lavender of the gown. She could never wear this gown in public, she decided with a feeling of regret.

"Faith," came the voice of the Countess through the open door between their rooms. "Come here. Let me see."

For a moment Faith hesitated. The Countess called again, this time more emphatically. "Faith!"

The habit of years was too strong for her. Faith moved obediently toward the next room.

"Ahhhh!" The Countess's eyes gleamed brightly from among her nest of pillows. "You are a beauty, my dear. Come closer."

Dutifully Faith approached the bed. "I – milady," she began.

"Hush, child," commanded the old woman. "Turn around and let me see the back."

Hesitantly Faith turned.

"Loosen the knot of your hair," commanded the Countess and Faith complied, her chestnut hair falling in a great cloud around her shoulders. Then she faced the Countess again.

The old woman was positively beaming. "My child, the dress does wonders for you." She shook her head. "That boy! His eye is always out for beauty. I swear he can see through any number of drab gowns."

"But milady – this gown! It's, it's unseemly. I can't go about like this."

"Like what?" demanded a deep voice from the doorway.

Faith's hands flew to her throat and she felt the scarlet flood her cheeks.

"Like what?" repeated his lordship, striding into the room.

Faith turned stricken eyes on the Countess, as though asking for help.

The old woman smiled at her nephew. "Faith is a little uncomfortable in such a gown. She thinks it may be unseemly."

"Unseemly!" The Earl's dark eyes flashed. "How can anything so beautiful be unseemly?"

Faith's cheeks grew even more heated. Perhaps the cheval glass had not lied. Perhaps she was beautiful. The thought was unnerving, very unnerving.

She looked at the Countess. "But – but it's so – bare!"

His lordship's dark eyes scrutinized her carefully. "I see that you have a throat and arms. Is it necessary that these parts of your anatomy be hidden from view?"

Faith was unable to answer. Those dark eyes seemed to hold her speechless.

"I assure you," continued his lordship, "that the gown is one of the most modest I have seen in some time."

"Modest!" Faith could not held exclaiming.

The Earl nodded. "I said modest and I mean modest. Just because the harridans with which you previously lived disliked beauty and clothed you in drabness that is no reason that the same stupidity must continue here."

Faith had no answer to this, nor did the Earl seem to expect one. He turned to his aunt. "You did well in choosing the pattern. And it fits her superbly."

The Countess nodded. "It does indeed, my boy. You have an excellent eye."

The Earl nodded. "Of course. I have had a great deal of practice."

He clothed his fancy women, Faith found herself thinking. That was why he knew so much about fashion. How many had he had? How many fancy women had felt the glow of those dark piercing eyes? And then as Faith realized to what extent her thoughts were taking her, she made a decided effort to stop

112

them. Fancy women indeed! His lordship's past was surely no concern of hers.

Silently she turned and began to move toward the door that led to her room. No matter what they said, she was extremely uncomfortable in this gown.

"Where do you think you are going?" His lordship swung suddenly to face her.

"I – I meant to change my gown," she stammered.

"Not now." His dark eyes seemed to mock her.

"Not now?" she repeated.

The Earl smiled laconically. "I hope your new gown has not marred your understanding. Do you not recall that when the gown was finished we were to have a walk on the moors?"

"I – I –" Faith wondered again why his lordship should have such a disquieting effect on her. It could not be the simple fact of his maleness. Mr. Felix did not have such an effect on her. Nor had Spacks nor the footmen nor the other butlers and footmen that she had known over the years. No, it was the Earl himself that she found so disturbing.

"Come," he commanded. "This is the day for our walk. Fetch a cloak." His eyes slid over her. "And do *not* change your gown. I wish to see if the material is a good match."

Faith bowed her head. "Yes, milord."

"And do not pin up your hair either," he continued. "I wish to see it blow in the wind."

Faith cast an anguished look at the Countess. "Milady?" she began.

"Go on, girl." The old woman waved a delicate hand. "I'll have Deevers up. Go on," she repeated as Faith still hesitated. "Go on and have a good time." There was something shining in the Countess's eyes, something Faith did not recognize. But it was obvious that her employer wanted her to walk with the Earl. It was equally obvious that she thought that her nurse-companion would be safe in the Earl's company.

Of this Faith was not so sure. She did not trust his lordship; she remembered the warnings issued by both Mr. Felix and Lady Clarisse. But one thing was clear to her. Her misgivings of the Earl had to do with the possibility of him making attempts – not on her life – but on her honor.

And, as Faith hurried to get the cloak, she wondered just how strong she would be in resisting should his lordship decided to kiss her again. The thought made the blood race to her face and throat.

She turned from the closet, cloak in hand, to find that the Earl had followed her. His presence in the room made her more nervous than ever. His virile maleness seemed out of place and threatening in this room where she slept and dressed.

"What, what do you want?" she asked.

The Earl's eyes mocked her but his tone was even. "I wish to go much farther afield today. Therefore some walking boots may be in order."

"Yes, milord." Faith turned again to the closet, conscious that his lordship's eyes were following her every move. She took out the pair of sturdy walking boots that were left from her days with Papa. They were scuffed and stained, but they fit.

The Earl's eyes were still upon her and Faith could not decide where to sit nor how to put on the boots.

"Such modesty," said his lordship dryly. "You act as though no man had ever seen your ankle."

"No man has," answered Faith, knowing that he would not believe her, but still compelled to say it.

"Then it is high time one did," replied his lordship. He advanced toward her.

Faith's heart rose up in her throat. She seemed unable to speak. As he took another step toward her she found herself taking a step backward. She was brought up sharply by the back of her knees hitting the side of the bed.

The Earl was very close now, his face only inches from her own. Surely he would not kiss her, not with his aunt in the next room. But she could not be sure.

While she stood there, trapped by the Earl's eyes, he reached out one strong brown hand and pushed her shoulder. Before she knew it, she was sitting on the bed and the Earl was kneeling before her. She was powerless to move as he removed her kid slippers and fastened the boots.

As in a dream she felt his fingers on her instep. As in a dream she looked down at the dark hair that curled around his collar. She wanted to reach out a hand and touch them, the dark unruly locks that were so like the man. But fear held her motionless, fear and a strange feeling that none of this could actually be real.

And then he had risen and extended his hand and, without thinking at all, she put her own hand in it and got to her feet. His lordship led her to the next room. "We are off on our walk, Aunt. I promise to bring Miss Duncan back with rosy cheeks and freshened lungs. *Adieu.*"

The old Countess chuckled. "Be nice to Faith, you rascal. And behave yourself.

Begone now and let an old woman rest."

As they made their way down the stairs, Faith felt as though she were in a dream. Never in those long days of servitude had she imagined wearing such a gown; never had she imagined walking at the side of such a man. And, the thought almost caused her to stumble, never had she imagined the kind of feelings that went surging through her at the mere sight of him.

As they reached the front door, Spack's moribund face preserved its glacial dignity, but his eyes seemed to have a questioning look. Faith had little time to consider the butler, however, for the Earl took her cloak from her lifeless fingers and fastened it carefully around her throat. As his fingers crept under the great mass of her hair to pull it from under the cloak, she felt that strange shiver of excitement down her spine.

Then his lordship pulled her arm through his and set off down the path toward the moors. "You are an admirable seamstress," he declared in a companionable tone. "The dress could have been made by London's leading dressmaker. You have many talents."

Faith raised her eyes at this last, but there appeared to be no mockery in his. And so she accepted the compliment as it seemed to be

117

meant. "Thank you, milord. You are most kind."

The Earl smiled. "You have been with us some days now. Tell me, how do you like it here?"

Faith was silent for some moments.

"Well?"

"I – I am taken aback," Faith replied. "No one has ever asked me how I liked a position. It is a rather strange thing."

The Earl shrugged. "Forget the past. Simply tell me about now."

Faith pondered as they continued to stroll along. "I like it here." She looked around her at the rolling expanse of heather-covered moorland. "I find it beautiful."

"And you are not lonely?"

"Lonely?" Surprise was evident in Faith's voice. "How could I be lonely? I have the Countess. She is the kindest employer I have ever known."

"Do you not find life rather dull, here away from the joys of London?"

Faith sighed; he still did not believe her. "Though you do not think so, milord, the joys of London were never known to me. Therefore I cannot miss them. I enjoy the company of the Countess. She is an exceedingly good conversationalist. My life is happier than it has ever been."

"And you do not long for excitement?"

"No, milord." Faith willed her voice not to reveal what her heart had just told her – that the most exciting thing in her life – and very exciting it was, too – was his lordship himself.

"And so you like the moors?"

"Yes, milord."

The Earl bent and picked a sprig of heather. He held it against her gown. "Almost a perfect match."

Faith, looking down at the little flowers, could only nod. It was most fortunate that his lordship could not know that in her room between the pages of her worn Bible there lay a sprig of heather very like that in his hand.

"You are a strange woman," his lordship observed as they continued on their way.

"How so, milord?" asked Faith. She could not help being curious about what he was thinking.

His lordship shrugged well-clad shoulders. "Sometimes I could almost swear you are the innocent you claim to be, but I know my brother. I know him well. And I cannot conceive to what end he would bring a real innocent here."

"I do not understand your antipathy toward Mr. Felix," said Faith. "He is such a gentle, mild-mannered man. Nor do I understand why I should be under suspicion. What is wrong with Mr. Felix hiring a nurse-companion for your aunt?"

The Earl scowled. "Either you are a very good actress or you are exceedingly naive. As the eldest son of the old Earl's brother – my father was already dead – I became the new Earl. Felix begrudged me the title, but even more he begrudges me the dowager Countess's private wealth. The Earldom and its assets came to me automatically. But what belongs privately to the Countess is hers to bequeath."

"I still do not understand."

"The matter is simple. My brother has imported more than one nurse-companion whose major task was to persuade my aunt to disinherit me."

"Milord! No nurse-companion would do such a thing."

"No legitimate one, perhaps. I have reason to believe that the women who preceded you were something else."

"And so you suspect *me?*" Faith stopped walking and turned to face him.

"Of course. Tell me truthfully. Did not my brother intimate to you that I would not grieve to see my aunt's early death?"

With sinking heart Faith recalled Mr. Felix's rather hesitant statement. "Yes, but he may well believe that. Such a different man from you. One who does not..." she paused, searching for words.

"If you mean that my brother does not keep fancy women and sit at the gaming tables," remarked his lordship with a mocking smile, "then you *are* an innocent. It is precisely because his debts have exhausted what our father left him that he is here, seeking to ingratiate himself with Aunt."

"But *you* are here." Faith was totally confused.

"Of course I am. Aside from the fact that Moorshead is mine, I do not care to have my aunt bamboozled by some cock-and-bull story. If you have any eyes at all, you have observed that she *loves* me. I do not wish her to believe that that love was foolishly given."

"But what if it was?" Faith found herself saying to her horror.

But the Earl did not seem angered. "I game and I pursue the women. Such is the life of a lord in this time. But neither of these marks me as an ungrateful churl who would forget the love lavished upon him in a lonely boyhood."

The Earl's eyes were dark and glittering. Before their penetrating gaze Faith's fell away.

"And so," observed his lordship with an enigmatic smile. "We have reached a stalemate. I cannot believe that you are really an innocent dupe of Felix's and you cannot believe that I am a man capable of loving."

"I did not say *that*," Faith protested.

"But you have thought it," replied his lordship. "I saw it in your eyes. They are most revealing."

Panic-stricken, she strove not to look at him, but some compulsion seemed to drag her eyes to his. His hands reached out to grab her shoulders. "For instance," he said, his face close to hers, "at this very moment those eyes of yours are speaking to me. They are begging me to kiss you."

"No! You are mistaken, milord."

"Truly?" The dark eyes mocked her as though he knew her true thoughts, knew that under the fear and anger was a desperate desire for the very kiss she denied wanting.

The Earl laughed harshly and put her from him. "Come," he said, "I have been too long alone with you. Your lips are most inviting."

A thought streaked through Faith's mind, a thought so painful that she flushed as though struck, but his lordship had turned away and so did not see. It had suddenly occurred to a mind unused to intrigue that his lordship had probably made advances to all those young women – and been accepted, no doubt. How else could he have been so completely confident that they were not what they claimed to be?

The kisses, the material for the gowns, the attention he had given her, would have been directed, no doubt, at whatever young woman currently filled her position. Well, she told herself, willing the tears to go away, none of this should be surprising. What other behavior could one expect from a rake? Indeed, none. He had one belief concerning women, their loyalties and their uses. To all other beliefs he was dead.

Faith took a deep breath as he tucked her arm once more through his own. She would simply have to get used to the idea, that was all. The Earl was a handsome charming man, and quite without scruples. From now on she would be doubly on guard against him.

They walked some little time in silence, Faith intent on putting down the treacherous tears that insisted on coming to her eyes.

Then his lordship spoke. "There is something else I wish to show you."

"What is it?" asked Faith, momentarily diverted from the pain of her discovery.

"You shall see. It does not bear description well." And he strode on.

The path led uphill and by degrees the heather fell away and was replaced by rock. By the time Faith reached the summit she was out of breath from the effort.

"Look," commanded the Earl.

"Oh!" Spread out below her lay miles and miles of heather-covered moorland. The sight was one of great beauty.

Faith moved from his side and approached the edge. Down below lay more rocks, great jagged boulders reaching high into the air. Faith shivered. To fall from this height would mean certain death.

She turned and found that the Earl had approached unheard and was directly behind her, so close that his outstretched hand brushed her shoulder as she turned. Panic grabbed at Faith's heart as that hand moved toward her. If he pushed her . . .

And then his fingers closed around her upper arm and he jerked her toward him. Her foot turned on a pebble and she stumbled, falling against him, which sent them both reeling backward down the slope. The Earl fell and she came to rest on top of him.

For long moments Faith fought to regain the breath that had been jarred from her body. And then she realized that she was lying on his lordship. And he was not moving!

Forgotten was her panic of moments before. Why wasn't he moving? Perhaps he had struck his head.

Carefully Faith eased herself to one side and peered at the silent face. "Milord," she cried. "Milord, are you hurt?"

There was no answer from the man lying so still beside her. Faith looked at him closely. There seemed to be no blood. But the awful stillness of him frightened her. If he were dead . . .

The force of her feelings came upon her so suddenly that she was hardly aware that she had put her lips to that still brow until after she had committed the terrible act. Before God, she must have lost her mind! But the fact was undeniable. She loved the Earl of Moorshead, loved him very much indeed.

Tears again filled her eyes and she put her ear anxiously to his chest. The steady beat of his heart was reassuring. If only he had not been hurt too badly.

The strain of the last few minutes began to tell on her and she let her head lie for a moment against his chest. And then she felt his arms come up to circle her. Faith looked up and met his eyes. "Milord, are you hurt?"

The Earl's eyes held something strange, an emotion she could not recognize.

"Yes. The rock is rather hard. But I believe nothing is broken. A lump on my head perhaps. And you?"

"I – I am all right. But I was concerned about you."

Faith tried to rise but, although his arms had released her, his hands had moved to her shoulders. Gently he pulled her up until her face was level with his. Her eyes seemed drawn to his lips. She closed her eyes, afraid of what he might be able to see there.

And then his lordship, with his arms still around her, rolled over very gently and she found herself beneath him, the long length of him pressing against her and her head cradled in his hands.

"Milo –" she began and then his lips found hers. She must fight him, she thought. He had no real feelings for her. He was taking unfair advantage. He was a rake, a man of no honor where women were concerned.

But all of her arguments with herself were futile, wiped from her consciousness by the gentle persuasion of lips that seemed to make rational thought impossible. Soon Faith was oblivious to everything but the waves of intense longing that forced her arms up to encircle his neck, her breath to come in great

126

gasps, and her body to experience sensations she had never known existed.

Chapter 9

The walk back to the castle was a quiet one. Both Faith and his lordship seemed lost in their thoughts. After the kiss he had courteously helped her to her feet and, without so much as a word of apology, tucked her arm through his and started the return journey.

Several times Faith had thought to remonstrate with him for that kiss, but the knowledge of her own yearning for it had put a bridle on her tongue. Perhaps he *had* seen the yearning in her eyes. She had no way of knowing. But at least covertly she was as guilty as he. For there was no denying her want, her intense, all-consuming wish to feel his lips on hers, his arms around her. Surely she could not blame *him* for that.

Finally they reached the great door and his lordship escorted her inside and left her with a bow. In bemusement she made her way up the great stairs to her room. There she removed her cloak, changed her shoes, and examined her gown for damage in the fall. There seemed to be none. She sighed, wishing for time to consider the events of the afternoon, but she could not, in good conscience, stay away from her duties any longer.

And so she moved on into the Countess's room. The Countess seemed to be resting easily and Faith took the opportunity to sit in idleness and examine her thoughts. They were thoughts in chaos, utter chaos. How could it have happened, that she should have formed a partiality for a man of his lordship's stamp? How could it have happened that she had so lost her senses?

At least an hour passed during which Faith sat in silent contemplation. But there were no answers to her questions. Finally she roused herself. The countess was sleeping overlong for a daytime nap.

She moved toward the bed. "Milady, milady," she called, but the Countess did not awaken. In panic Faith bent to listen to the Countess's heart. It was beating. The old woman was alive, but something was wrong. Usually she slept lightly and was quite easily awakened.

Gently and then more harshly, she shook the Countess. Finally the old eyes opened a little. "Faith. Don't feel well."

Faith expelled a sigh of relief. "There now. Just lie still." She hurried to the basin and dipped in a cloth. Gently she laved the old woman's brow.

"Thank you, Faith. I'm feeling better now." The Countess sighed. "My sleep was so heavy today, heavy and yet troubled."

"I thought Deevers was going to sit with you," said Faith. Suspicion was rearing its ugly head. The Countess had been in fine spirits when Faith left her. And now, now she seemed so listless, so worn out, almost as though someone had drugged her!

Faith had never been employed by anyone who used such things, but occasionally she had heard the maids and footmen whispering about their former masters. There had been whispers of strange goings-on in other households. Strange concoctions had changed masters into strangers who said weird things and behaved in a peculiar fashion, sometimes appearing to be almost dead in their lethargy.

"Where is Deevers? When did she leave you?" asked Faith.

The Countess shook her head weakly. "I sent her back to her duties when I decided to nap."

"Did you eat or drink?" asked Faith, trying to keep her voice even.

"Only some water," said the Countess.

"Nothing that would disagree with my stomach."

Faith nodded. She was glad the Countess had misinterpreted her question. It was not an accidental ingestion of some food that Faith feared, but someone's deliberate tampering with the Countess's food or drink. Was it possible that someone had added something to them?

The Countess managed a faint smile. "Faith, my dear, do not look so concerned. I just had a bad sleep." She shuddered. "Such nightmares! Strange monsters and the like. It's been years since I've dreamed of such horrors."

"Perhaps we should summon the doctor," Faith suggested.

"No, indeed," replied the Countess, her voice gaining strength. "There's no sense in the poor man having the long journey out here just because an old woman has had some bad dreams. Besides, I want you to sew on your other gowns. Find Deevers and get her to help you cut out the green one."

"But milady —"

"Go," said the Countess.

"I'll just bring you some fresh water, too," said Faith, grabbing the glass and pitcher and hurrying out.

As she made her way toward the kitchen

wing the dark shadows in the corridors seemed to be reaching out for her. It was not ghosts that she feared Faith told herself, but humans. It hardly seemed possible that anyone would want to hurt the Countess. And yet, Mr. Felix had warned her about his lordship. And his lordship and aunt had warned her about Mr. Felix. And all three of them had warned her about the Lady Clarisse.

She could not believe that his lordship meant harm to his aunt. And yet he was the only one who stood to gain anything if her illness became fatal. And he had been alone in the room with her when he sent Faith for her cloak.

It was just too difficult for her, she thought, as she reached the kitchen. The old house-keeper looked up as Faith entered. "Hello, Deevers," Faith tried to keep her voice even.

"Hello, miss." Deever's smile reflected her acceptance of Faith.

"Was anyone in to visit the Countess while I was gone?"

Deevers shook her head. "No, miss. Mr. Felix, he don't visit her often. Nor Lady Clarisse. Their visits aggravates her."

Faith nodded. "And so she sent you out when she decided to nap?"

"Aye, miss. Is something wrong?"

Faith frowned. "The Countess isn't feeling

131

well. And I can't understand it. You must not breathe a word of this to anyone else, understand?"

"Oh no, miss! I wouldn't." Deever's eyes grew wide.

"I suspect that someone may have put something in her water."

"Miss!"

"It's only a suspicion, Deevers. Perhaps living here has unsettled my nerves. But let us be extra careful."

"Oh yes, miss. Yes, indeed." Deevers's gray head nodded in complete agreement. "I'll wash them out real good, miss. And I'll watch."

It was not until she was making her way back through the shadows that Faith realized that she had hoped to have Deevers chase away her fears. But Deevers hadn't; the old housekeeper had not even tried to suggest that such a thing was impossible.

Faith sighed. Not too long ago the worst thing in her life had been the angry scoldings of an old shrew. Suddenly that seemed almost pleasant in contrast to the complexities that life now held for her. How was she, an unsophisticated young woman with little knowledge of men and their ways, to decide which of the brothers was guilty? And even that seemed impossible considering that she

132

could not be sure that anyone had done anything to be guilty of.

As she hurried back to the Countess, she grew increasingly aware of a strange tingling sensation in her scalp, as though someone was watching her. Once she even stopped abruptly and turned to look behind her. But of course there was no one there. Her nerves, she thought, were becoming quite frayed.

Being constantly so close to the Earl – it was, after all, impossible for her to avoid his visits to his aunt or dinner with him at the table – had already made her jump at the slightest sound and color up whenever looked at. This was very unlike her old self, very unlike indeed.

And now she was faced with these horrid suspicions. And there was very little she could do about them. But in good conscience she could not disregard them, not if the Countess's life might be endangered.

By the time Faith went down to dinner she had composed herself to some degree and was able to meet the glances of the Earl and Mr. Felix without flinching. And she was able to make ordinary conversation with them.

Several times during the meal she thought that his lordship was looking at her strangely, but perhaps, she told herself, perhaps it was only her imagination. That faculty, she feared, had been sadly overused these past days. The ancient castle with its dark gloomy corridors, this talk of ghosts and secret passageways, and, worst of all, her terrible suspicions of the two men, had left her unable to decide what was reality and what was not.

The meal was over and Faith was preparing to return to her duties, when his lordship spoke. "I have a matter to discuss with you in the library," he said to Faith.

Lady Clarisse looked at him with startled gray eyes. "But, Hugh –"

"This is a matter of business, Lady Clarisse, and will take but a few minutes. Come, Miss Duncan."

Obediently Faith rose and followed his lordship down the hall and into the library. He closed the door behind her and turned to face her. "Now – what is this that Deevers is telling me?"

Faith felt herself coloring up. "I asked her not to say anything to anyone," she stammered.

"Deevers thought that I would be interested in my aunt's welfare, even if you didn't," replied his lordship angrily.

"But – but it wasn't that," said Faith. "I have only suspicions."

"What are they?" demanded the Earl, fixing her with an angry eye.

"Before we left," Faith said, "the Countess was fine – alert and bright."

The Earl nodded. "Yes, I know."

"When I returned to her room she was sleeping. I – I sat for some time and she did not awaken. It was unlike her to sleep so long and so heavily during the day. Finally I woke her. It was very difficult. She looked strange. Her eyes were glazed and dull. She reported having very bad dreams. About monsters and strange creatures."

"And this frightened you?"

Faith nodded. "I have heard of things – potions that cause strange dreams."

"In your innocent past, I suppose."

This was no time for sarcasm and Faith chose to ignore his. "It was from one of Mrs. Petrie's footmen. He had once worked for a lord who was fond of a certain drug. He smoked it in some sort of pipe."

"Opium," said his lordship.

"Yes, that was the name of it. And he spoke of other drugs. I do not remember their names. But the Countess seemed so different, especially her eyes."

"I see. Have you mentioned this to anyone but Deevers?"

"No, milord."

"Do not. Promise me this, Faith." His eyes burned into hers. "If anyone else hears of this, you will be in great danger."

She looked at him in amazement. "Danger? I?"

"Yes! Your promise."

She hesitated and he took her hands in his. "I still do not know if you are the innocent you claim to be," he said. "But I do know that you would not harm my aunt. And *if* someone is drugging her, and *if* that someone discovers that you know it, you will be in danger. I am much too fond of you to want that."

Faith, staring into those gleaming eyes, felt the man's great power. It was foolish of her to suspect him, she told herself. "I promise."

"Good. Now return to Aunt. I have instructed Deevers to prepare all the food herself. You must keep an eye on the water pitcher when guests are present."

"Yes, milord." Faith found that her bottom lip was trembling.

The Earl pressed the hands that were still clasped between his own. "Don't be afraid, Faith. I will see that you come to no harm. And I will protect Aunt, too. Now, away with you."

For another long moment Faith looked

into his eyes and then, fearful of what hers might reveal, she lowered them and turned away.

She thought of that scene again as she lay in bed later that night. Why was it that his eyes seemed to paralyze her in that way? What was the secret of the Earl's power? She pondered these questions for some moments and then, unable to find any answers, reluctantly allowed her thoughts to return to the possible causes of the Countess's condition. This, too, proved a fruitless endeavor and she tossed and turned, unable to relax, her ears alert for any sound from the adjoining room. She had left the door open so that she could hear should the Countess call for her. But gradually fatigue overcame her. It had been a very long day. The walk on the moor and the excitement of seeing the Countess so dull and dazed had taken their toll, and so her eyelids fluttered lower and lower.

And then suddenly a long drawn-out wail sounded through the hall and Faith sat bolt upright in the bed. My God! What could be making that awful noise?

As Faith shivered in the bed, the sound of sobs reached her ears. She clutched herself. Sobs! And right outside her door. Could it be possible? Could the ghost be walking? After

137

all, the moon was full. Its light streamed in through the high windows.

Of course not, she told herself firmly. She did not believe in ghosts. But the fact was inescapable – someone was crying outside her door. And it sounded very much like a woman.

Suddenly Faith grew angry. She was tired of this castle and all its mysteries. If someone – ghost or not – were crying out there in the hall, she intended to see who it was. With this resolve firmly in mind she pushed back the covers and swung her feet onto the floor. The stone was icy but Faith had no time to grope for slippers. Silently she made her way to the door.

She was halfway there when the sobbing ceased. Hurriedly she covered the remaining distance and flung open the heavy door. There was no one there, but down the hall there was a splash of white against the shadows. Without more thought Faith set out after it. She would put this ghost business to an end.

The great hall was lit only by an occasional candle in a wall sconce but the figure moved swiftly. Whoever it was, the "apparition" knew its way well, she thought bitterly as she hurried after it.

She followed it past the Countess's closed

door and on through the shadowed corridor. Faith wished that more candles had been left burning. All she could see was the vague outline of a white-clad figure, and no matter how she hurried, it seemed to stay an equal distance ahead of her.

Her feet were like blocks of ice on the cold stone floor and her teeth chattered in her head, but she would not give up the pursuit. It must stop sometime, somewhere. And then she would see.

And then the ghost reached that part of the castle which was closed off. Faith saw it go through a door that was always kept locked. In the darkness she could not see if the door had been open or if the ghost had really gone "through" it.

She swallowed. It was very dark in the deserted part of the castle. There would be no candles burning there. And it was out of everyone's hearing. In the dark shadows by the now closed door, she hesitated. Then suddenly a hand was clasped over her mouth and an arm went around her waist. In the darkness Faith fought wildly, using every ounce of strength, but a hard arm pressed her tight against him and the Earl whispered in her ear, "Sssh, Faith. It's me."

Her relief was so overwhelming that she went limp against him. He released her mouth

139

then and she whispered, "The door. It has gone though the door. We must follow it. See who it is."

The Earl shook his head. "No, we must *not* follow it."

"But I want to know," Faith said, conscious that she was beginning to tremble.

The Earl shook her lightly. "Hush." Then he lifted her easily into his arms and turned back the way she had come.

"Milord!" protested Faith.

"Quiet!" he commanded sternly and she obeyed.

It was strange being carried through the dark shadowed halls with her arms around the Earl's neck. And she wore nothing but her nightdress! The thought brought the blood to her face.

Gradually she grew conscious of the beating of his heart under her ear and the warmth of his body against her cold one. She realized, too, that he was fully dressed and it was quite late.

She kept the silence he had insisted on until they had reached the door to her room. There she struggled to be released, but his lordship paid her no heed.

While Faith's heart rose in her throat, he crossed the room in great strides and deposited her on the bed. Then he sat beside

140

her and, while she watched in horror, his hands went to the hem of her nightdress. "Milord!" cried Faith.

"Your feet are like ice," he said calmly, chafing them between warm hands. "You will grow ill like this."

For a few moments all was silent except for the sound of the Earl's hands moving on her feet. Finally he was satisfied and released them. He rose, pulled the covers over her, then reseated himself. "Now," he said seriously, "we will talk. Tell me what happened."

As precisely as she could Faith recounted the wail and the sobs and her decision to discover the perpetrator.

His lordship scowled. "Did I not warn you against pursuing ghosts into the shadows?"

"Yes, but –"

The Earl laid a finger on her lips. "You are a foolhardy young woman. In the future I expect you to stay in your warm bed. Do you understand?"

"But who could be doing such a thing?"

"Perhaps there *are* ghosts in this house," replied his lordship darkly. "At any rate, stay out of the shadows and the parts of the castle that are shut off. Agreed?"

His eyes held hers. "Agreed," she replied solemnly. "Oh! The Countess!"

She was about to rise once more when he pushed her down. "Stay where you are. I'll check."

Faith's heart pounded in her throat as he moved off. She was frightened. There was no doubt of that. But of whom or of what she wasn't quite sure.

In moments the Earl returned. "She is fine, sleeping well. There is no further cause for concern. Go back to sleep."

Faith shook her head. "I – I can't."

"You must," said his lordship sternly. "There's no need to fear. I shall be in the next room and can hear you call. And remember, no more chasing ghosts."

His eyes gleamed brightly in the moonlight. "Thank you, milord," Faith murmured. She did not want him to go, yet she dared do nothing to keep him with her. For if he looked too long into her eyes, would he not see that now she was breathing so heavily not because of the ghost, but because of him? Would he not see, as he had seen before, that she desired his kiss? At the thought she averted her gaze.

"Good night, Faith," said his lordship softly.

"Good night, milord."

"Your new nightdress," said the Earl, "is quite becoming."

"Oh!" Her eyes sought his face in confusion and she clutched the covers to her.

The Earl smiled mischievously. "Too late, my dear. I have already had a good view. You may chastise me tomorrow. For tonight, sleep."

And then he was gone. Faith heard the slight creak as he opened the door to the room on the left. She sighed. It gave her great comfort to know that the Earl was within calling distance and that the Countess was safe.

Suddenly Faith's hands clutched at each other. But *was* the Countess safe? She had only the Earl's word for it. And – and he *was* suspect.

Softly she drew back the covers and put her feet to the floor. The iciness made her shiver but she stole softly into the Countess's room, heard her breathing normally, and returned satisfied to her own bed.

Surely she was wrong to mistrust him, she thought. She felt so safe with him. And yet history was undoubtedly replete with examples of women who had felt safe in a man's arms, been left helpless by the strength of his kisses, and lived to rue the day. Or did not!

The chill seemed to move up from Faith's feet and attack her whole body. Did the Earl

143

really want to kill her? There *had* been the occasion on the cliffs this afternoon, but he had saved her then. And he had saved her again tonight, unless ... Could there be some reason that he did not want her in the other part of the castle? Could he be in league with the ghost?

For some time Faith tossed and turned, and as exhaustion finally overcame her, she drifted off into slumber. But it was not a peaceful slumber. Far from it. Her dreams were haunted by ghosts and nightmare scenes of the old Earl chasing his screaming wife to the cliff's edge. And then, finally, toward morning, those gave way to more peaceful ones and she dreamed she was sleeping, warm and snug in her new nightdress in the arms of the present Earl.

Chapter 10

Faith's first act on waking the next morning was to thrust her feet hurriedly into her slippers and run in to the Countess. The old woman opened her eyes and smiled. "My dear girl, you will catch a chill running around like that. Whatever are you thinking of?"

Faith was covered with confusion but she did not return to her room for a robe. "Last night I heard the ghost," she said hurriedly.

"I hope you stayed snugly in your bed," observed the Countess with a strange twinkle in her eye.

Faith shook her head. "No, I followed it."

The old woman frowned. "That was unwise, Faith. Do not do it again."

"That's what he sa –" The color flooded Faith's cheeks at the renewed realization that his lordship had seen her in her nightdress. Seen her and carried her!

"You needn't turn so fiery red, child." The Countess chuckled. "I was awake when Hugh brought you back to your room."

"Did *you* hear the ghost?"

The Countess shook her head. "No. Perhaps that was what woke me, but I have no recollection of it. But I saw Hugh when he came to be sure I was safe. I saw you, too."

"I – I wanted to be sure," Faith faltered.

The Countess's face took on an expression of sadness. "You do not trust Hugh, do you?"

"I – I don't know." Faith wrung her hands. "Everyone seems to mistrust everyone and –"

"Come, do not hesitate," the Countess urged. "What were you told about Hugh?"

"I – I –"

"Tell me," commanded the Countess. "Do not be concerned for my feelings."

Faith took a deep breath. "I was told that his lordship – that he needed money – for gambling debts." She paused, unsure how to continue.

"And you were told that he would not be too upset should I depart this life prematurely, so to speak."

Faith could only nod. How could the Countess lie there and speak so calmly of such things?

The Countess smiled curtly. "I am an old woman. I do not even mind dying. But Hugh, my Hugh, would not hurt me. I know that." Her eyes shone with unshed tears. "If I *believed* such a thing, I should *wish* to be dead. But I do not," she added crisply. "And I never will."

"But –" Faith wanted to believe the Countess, to allay the suspicions of his lordship that rose periodically to haunt her, but the Countess could be mistaken. "Men do change. Gambling debts. Fancy women."

The Countess laughed. "Hugh has been on the town for some time. And, in spite of his devilish good looks and his insatiable appetite for excitement, he has a sound head on his shoulders. I simply will not believe ill of him."

"Yes, milady," Faith fully respected the Countess's feelings. She thought that she, too, might want to die if she discovered that his lordship was anxious to hasten his aunt's death.

The thought occurred to her to ask why Mr. Felix should tell such horrid things about his brother. But the subject was bound to be a painful one for the old woman and so Faith remained silent.

"Has Hugh been harassing you?" asked the Countess with a little smile.

Faith shook her head. "Oh no, milady." That was not a lie. His lordship had not harassed her. The fact that she found his presence so disturbing was surely not his fault. And that kiss – when they had fallen onto the rock together – that could not be called harassing.

The Countess chuckled. "I collect from the way you color up at his appearance here that my nephew's charm is apparent to you."

Faith was shamed, but she made her answer truthful. "Yes, milady. His lordship is most disconcerting to me, I am sorry to say."

The Countess smiled. "No need to be ashamed, my girl. It would take a woman of iron to withstand such a man. A woman stronger than you or I."

Faith could only nod. It was most fortunate,

she told herself, that the Countess was such an understanding person. She attempted to voice her thanks. "Milady, you have been so kind to me. I hardly know how to thank –"

"Nonsense," replied the Countess crisply. "I am not so old that I cannot remember what youth is like." Her black eyes rested on Faith's flushed face. "I told you that I came out. I did not tell you that all I had was my youth and beauty, that my Papa had wasted his substance at the gaming table and so I had no dowry to speak of." The old eyes glittered with emotion. "If I hadn't met my Henry, and if he hadn't loved me enough to forgo the dowry, I might very well have ended up like you. Or as the wife of some lustful, decrepit old man." The Countess sighed. "Henry's money meant nothing to me, nothing whatsoever. It was the man himself that I loved."

She gave Faith a reassuring smile. "I do not judge people by their financial wealth, but by their character. That is why I am so fond of you. You are a good girl, Faith, a really good girl."

Faith felt the tears rise to her eyes and blinked rapidly. No one of her previous employers had ever spoken to her in kindly tones or treated her as a person with feelings. They had all seen her as a slave to be shouted

148

at, ordered about, and generally abused.

"Now child, don't go teary on me," said the Countess briskly. "I collect you've had more than your share of trouble in this life. Now run along and dress before you catch a chill. I want you to work on the green gown today. I'm anxious to see you in it."

"Yes, milady." Faith attempted no more thanks, but hurried back to her room to wash and dress. As she did so she breathed a silent prayer of thanksgiving. It seemed that the loss of her position with Mrs. Petrie, which at first had appeared to be a calamity, was in fact a golden opportunity. Certainly life had never been this good before.

Of course, the appearance of the ghost and the enmity between the Earl and his brother, to say nothing of the Earl's disturbing influence on her, were all threats to the continued existence of that good life. But she would deal with one thing at a time. That had been her habit in the past and it had sustained her so far. It would help her deal with the future.

The day passed pleasantly. The Countess was again in good spirits and Faith felt hopeful that in a few days she might be moved to a chair for short periods of time.

The Countess was rather doubtful. "I don't

know, my dear. I haven't been out of this bed now for a long time. My legs won't support me."

Faith smiled. "I'm sure Deevers and I can manage to make you comfortable."

The Countess smiled too. "You have a way about you, Faith. And I have gotten much stronger since you've been here."

She grinned. "Part of it, I suppose, is due to your forcing me into better eating habits. Well, if you say so, we shall try it."

"It will only be for a short while, milady. And I'm sure you'll enjoy it. But for now, shall I read to you?"

The Countess shook her head. "No, work on that green gown. I've a desire to see you in it. After your wearing the rose-lavender yesterday that drab thing you've got on now looks even worse. I'll be pleased when you've got them all made and can throw those old things away."

Faith nodded. "Yes, milady." She was conscious that she had been loathe to put on the old gown, but she was saving the heather one – as *he* had called it – to wear to dinner.

And so the day wore on. Faith stitched steadily away, dreaming of how she would look in this gown when it was finished.

Sometimes the Countess dozed lightly and sometimes she recalled the times of her

150

girlhood or the golden days of her marriage. "Oh, we had our differences, Henry and I. But we always *knew* that our love was strong enough to overcome anything. And it was. Even death did not destroy my love for him."

The Countess turned gleaming black eyes on Faith. "I am quite ready to go, you see. For I believe that Henry is waiting for me. But I do not want my departure to leave any cloud of suspicion hanging over Hugh. And I would very much like to see the boy find a true love before I leave him."

It seemed unlikely to Faith that his lordship would ever know real love, the kind that *was* a woman's whole existence, but she did not voice her doubt because it would be painful to the Countess.

"You must go soon and dress for dinner," said the Countess. "You do plan to wear the rose-lavender, don't you?"

"Yes, milady."

"Good. Very good."

For a moment Faith wondered why the Countess should take such an interest in what she wore to dinner, but then she dismissed the thought. The Countess simply had very little to brighten her life and so took pleasure in trivial things.

And so, when she had washed and slipped on the heather dress, she returned to give the Countess a look.

"Excellent. Oh, excellent. Had your father had the sense and the resources to bring you out, you would have taken the *ton* by storm."

"Oh, milady!"

"It's the truth," replied the Countess crisply. "There's not a thing wrong with my eyes. Haven't you looked in your cheval glass?"

"Yes, milady, but –"

"But nothing," said the Countess firmly. "There's no sense disputing what is obvious. And if you don't believe *me*, just watch Clarisse's face when she sees you in that gown. If she doesn't turn positively green with envy, I miss my guess."

Faith could not help smiling at such a word picture, but she was still nervous. That his lordship had approved of her gown was obvious. But what would Mr. Felix say to all these new gowns?

So much had been happening that she had not given much consideration to Mr. Felix's words about the question he intended to ask her. But if he were talking about marriage – and that certainly seemed likely – then she should be giving the matter some thought.

Habituated by her years of service, she found it difficult to imagine herself as anyone's wife. But, if Mr. Felix offered ... He was, after all, a kind and gentle man. It was true that he did not leave her breathless and trembling as his lordship did. But he seemed a sound, substantial man. She could not give much credence to the Earl's charge that his brother was also a rake and a gambler. Mr. Felix simply did not have the look of such a man.

"Faith!" The Countess was staring at her.

"Yes, milady?"

The Countess smiled. "Well, take yourself off to dinner. Take your time and enjoy yourself. I shall be fine."

Faith smiled as she turned to leave the room, but the smile had faded before she reached the great stone staircase. She was fearful of meeting the Earl's eyes, fearful of what he could see in hers. But, she told herself, she could not avoid the man and so she must simply learn not to be so affected by him.

A sudden thought made her pause halfway down the stairs. Perhaps marriage to Mr. Felix was the answer to the vexing problem of the Earl. Surely his lordship would not pursue his brother's wife. He would return to London and she and Mr. Felix would remain to care for the Countess. But then it was difficult to predict *what* his lordship might do.

As she neared the dining room she heard the voices of the others and her knees began to tremble. She took a deep breath. There was no sense in avoiding the inevitable. Difficult things were best done as soon as possible, before a person was overcome by fear.

Quietly she stepped through the door and went to join the others. His lordship was facing in her direction and so he was the first to see her." Good evening, Miss Duncan." His eyes swept over her admiringly, but he made no comment.

Faith was attempting not to color up when Mr. Felix and Lady Clarisse both turned to regard her. Mr. Felix's face broke into a gentle smile of pleasure, but the lady's eyes turned cold as ice.

Faith kept her own expression even and pleasant and returned Mr. Felix's smile. How strange that a woman with Lady Clarisse's beauty should be so jealous of an inconsequential companion. But then, Faith told herself, she had never been able to understand women like Lady Clarisse. Certainly money was a necessity of life and could make that life much more enjoyable. But to sell herself to an old, worn-out rake for the sake of his title and possessions – this was something Faith could not countenance. Far better the kind of life she had led. It was at least decent and clean.

"Your new gown is quite charming," said Mr. Felix, offering her his arm.

"Thank you," Faith replied, noting rather absently that something had just caused the Earl to scowl fiercely.

But she had little time to consider his actions, for Mr. Felix was leading her to the table and Lady Clarisse had attached herself to the Earl and was smiling up at him. Faith directed her attention to Mr. Felix. There was certainly little point in being upset by the actions of Lady Clarisse. If the lady chose to think that she had a claim on the Earl, then that was the lady's problem. She was quite likely, though, thought Faith with a feeling of triumph which was entirely unbefitting one of her station, to be greatly disappointed in the Earl. He was not, Faith felt certain, ever going to put his title or his fortune into the lovely, grasping hands of the beautiful Lady Clarisse. He was far too worldly not to discover her true character. It was as the Countess had said; it simply pleased him to amuse himself with the lady.

Mr. Felix seated her in her usual place and settled beside her. "I hope that my aunt furnished you with stuff for more dresses. This one is quite pleasant to the eye."

"Yes, sir," replied Faith, conscious of the Earl's dark eyes upon her. "There was a great deal of material. The Countess has been very kind to me."

Mr. Felix's expression did not change, but Lady Clarisse's brittle laughter rang out and her cold gray eyes challenged Faith. "Come, Miss Duncan, there is no need to tell us a clanker like that. We all know the old woman is a witch, impossible to live with. I'm just thankful *I* don't have to live in such close proximity to her."

Faith felt a surge of unfamiliar anger. "I am sorry to contradict you, milady, but the Countess is a very kind woman. Not in the least a – witch."

Faith refused to lower her eyes before the onslaught of those cold gray ones. She refused to sit quietly by and let Lady Clarisse say such cutting things about the Countess.

"I cannot understand what you hope to gain by refusing to admit how the old woman is," Lady Clarisse continued. "Certainly we all know the truth about her. God knows, we have been on the receiving end of her razor tongue more than once."

Faith lips tightened grimly. "I am sorry to contradict your ladyship again, but I must insist. The Countess has never raised her voice to me. Not once. Nor has she ever been cross with me."

Even Mr. Felix seemed a little disturbed by this statement and silence hung heavy in the room.

Finally his lordship spoke. "I suggest that we drop the subject. Perhaps Miss Duncan's experience of Aunt has been different from ours because *she* is different. At any rate, we must let her continue in her beliefs. I doubt that we can change them."

Faith heard his words with a certain sense of disbelief. Why didn't *he* defend his aunt? But after this suggestion, he again turned his attention to his roast beef and everyone followed suit. Faith found her appetite quite suddenly diminished, but she automatically continued to eat.

They had reached the pastries before conversation began again and then it was Mr. Felix who spoke. "The moon is full tonight. I wonder if the ghost will be walking?"

Lady Clarisse shivered and clutched at the Earl's arm. "Oh Hugh, I should feel so much safer if your room were next to mine."

"Nonsense," said his lordship. And, though his eyes seemed to slide carelessly over Faith she clearly understood that she was not to mention where he had slept the night before. "You simply remain in your bed. The ghost has never harmed anyone who did not follow it."

"Well, perhaps we shall not see the ghost at all this month," observed Mr. Felix.

His lordship's eyes met Faith's again briefly and she knew somehow what she was to do. "The ghost was about last night," she said. "I heard her."

"Oh!" Lady Clarisse again clutched at his lordship's arm, and Faith thought how foolish the woman looked.

"I hope you were not unduly frightened," said Mr. Felix with grave concern, leaning over to pat her bare arm. Again his lordship's brows drew together in a dark scowl.

"No," said Faith. "Indeed, I even saw it. I set out to follow, but I had forgotten my slippers and the floor was too cold. So I returned to my bed."

"My word," said Mr. Felix. "You must never undertake such a foolhardy thing again."

"Yes, sir," replied Faith. "I found it quite a useless venture anyway as I could not seem to catch up."

"Of course not," said his lordship calmly. "Ghosts may only be seen up close when *they* wish it."

"Perhaps you are right, milord," replied

Faith with a small smile. "But, at any rate, if the ghost wishes to walk about again, it will not be hampered by me."

"A very wise decision," commented his lordship dryly. And Faith wondered how it was that she could know with such absolute certainty that this night and for nights to come, his lordship would be occupying the room next to hers. But she did know it.

"Did the ghost disappear into the wall or something?" asked Lady Clarisse, apparently unwilling to let go of a subject that offered her so much opportunity to hang on his lordship.

"No, milady," said Faith. "It went into the closed-off part of the castle."

Mr. Felix frowned. "It was certainly wise of you not to follow it there. And was my aunt disturbed by this?"

"No, sir," replied Faith. "She did not hear it."

"That's just as well," sighed Mr. Felix. "It would be extremely frightening to the dear old lady."

Faith suddenly devoted herself to the pastry in front of her. Mr. Felix had always been so kind and gentle with her. From their first meeting he had been pleasant and friendly. Witness his sending the coach for her and all the nice little attentions he had shown her since her arrival, treating her more like an equal than an employee.

But he certainly was mistaken about his aunt. He hardly seemed to know her at all. Surely someone who had been at all close to the Countess would realize that she would not be frightened by a ghost. And to refer to her as a dear old lady in that tone of voice, that was unlike Mr. Felix.

Faith choked suddenly on a piece of pastry as she kept back a chuckle. If ever Mr. Felix had referred to his aunt in her hearing with words such as those, he would surely have met with a sharp retort. Dear old lady, indeed!

She cast a look at his lordship, to see if he appreciated the humor of such a thing, but he, too, seemed devoted to his pastry.

Faith experienced a suddenly lurching in the vicinity of her stomach as Lady Clarisse wiped her red mouth very daintily and plucked at his lordship's sleeve. "You did promise to read me some more Byron, Hugh. You have such a lovely voice. So deep. So expressive."

Really, thought Faith, the lady's machinations were quite sickening at times. Couldn't she tell that such things would be of far more value if his lordship did the suggesting?

And then she smiled at herself. Imagine

her, a nurse-companion with no experience of men, thinking that she knew better than a lady how to handle a man of his lordship's ilk. And yet, his lordship *had* seemed attracted to her. And he did not seem excessively pleased with Lady Clarisse's attentions. Indeed, he removed her hand from his sleeve. "I have been rather out of sorts lately and believe I shall retire early as I did last night."

Faith forced her face to remain expressionless. It had been quite late last night when his lordship had carried her back to her room. It had been quite late and he had been fully clothed. For whatever reason he had retired early the previous evening it had not been to seek his bed.

"I suggest," his lordship continued smoothly, "that you and Felix entertain each other for this once. Perhaps Miss Duncan will join you."

Lady Clarisse made a face at his first suggestion and she obviously did not like the second any better. For one brief moment Faith was tempted to make the lady even more uncomfortable by agreeing. But the prospect of any length of time in the lady's company was just too unpleasant. "No thank you, milord, I must return to my duties."

"Of course." The Earl's tone was completely noncommittal and his eyes did not seem to be mocking her. Yet it was difficult to be sure.

Faith rose from the table. "Good night," she said and received replies from the others.

As she made her way back to the great staircase, now shrouded in deep shadows, Faith wondered again about his lordship. Had the Countess's previous companions really been of the sort he claimed? Surely he was mistaken. After all, just because they had succumbed to his lordship, given in to him – her breath came short at the thought – that needn't mean that they were fancy women. If they were sheltered and innocent as she had been, it could very well be that they had not been able to resist him. The Earl was a man of great power, that was certain. And she surmised that it was not often he failed to get what he wanted from a woman.

Sometime later, having recounted the various reactions to her adventure of the night before to the Countess's satisfaction and having settled her for the night, Faith returned to her own room. In the light of the single candle the room seemed huge and full of shadows. Faith found herself wishing that the night were not so cloudy. The light of the moon would be most welcome.

She had locked the Countess's door – the

one that led to the hall – and now she checked her own. Yes, it too, was locked. As she moved back toward the great bed she was very grateful for the open door that connected her room to that of the Countess. She supposed that it was rather silly, but the knowledge that the Countess would hear her should she call out was quite comforting.

Faith slipped out of the rose-lavender gown and hung it carefully in the wardrobe. She should have the green one finished soon. Then she pulled her nightdress over her head and loosened the coil of her hair. The shadows in the room were somehow threatening and Faith climbed into the bed to brush her hair.

As yet she had not heard his lordship moving in the next room. Perhaps she had been mistaken, but the certainty that his lordship was near at hand and would protect her did not leave her mind.

There was a tap on the door between the rooms. "Come in," called Faith softly, clutching the covers.

The door opened to disclose his lordship. He was still completely dressed and he smiled at her. "Surely you do not believe that I would attack you with Aunt in the next room," he whispered.

Faith shook her head, but she did not release her grip on the covers.

His lordship moved closer. "I came to tell you not to be afraid. I shall spend the night in the next room. And you," he looked down at her sternly. "You are not to leave your bed. Do you understand?"

"Yes, milord." Faith could not seem to tear her eyes away from his. The candle flickered in their dark depths – and something else. Faith felt herself being drawn toward him. If she could just snuggle into his arms as she had in her dreams, just lie there snugly against his chest and not have to think about anything except how good it felt.

"Lie back," whispered his lordship with a mischievous smile.

Hesitantly, Faith obeyed. Beneath the covers that she still clutched in nervous fingers her body trembled. But it was not fear that caused her to react so. She did not fear the Earl, she told herself. Rather, she feared her own attraction to him.

As his lordship sat down on the edge of the bed, Faith found that she was holding her breath. He was so near. And she must not, dared not, make a move toward him. She hardly dared look at him. For if he should glimpse in her eyes the depth of her feeling for him . . .

Gently his lordship reached out and disengaged the covers from her still trembling fingers. "Your hands are cold," he said, raising them, one after the other, to his lips. And then he lifted the covers and put them gently by her sides. On each hand was a burning spot where his lips had touched her flesh.

His lordship's eyes rested momentarily on the tucked top of her nightdress that was rising and falling in time to her madly thudding heart. It seemed to Faith as though she lay naked under those searching eyes. He pulled the covers up under her chin.

"Sleep well," he said softly. "And do not be afraid."

Faith could not answer for the constriction that his nearness had caused in her throat. Then he was looking once more into her eyes and Faith dropped her lashes. It *must* be apparent to him – her desperate longing for his kiss. She half expected to feel his lips pressing on hers. But instead she felt his hand brush the hair from her forehead. Just so gently, so tenderly, might a man touch his beloved wife, thought Faith, conscious that a deep feeling of contentment had stolen over her.

She sighed peacefully. Strange that a man such as the Earl should inspire so much trust. Perhaps she would dream again of being in his arms.

Chapter 11

Several days passed. Faith stitched diligently on the green dress, but her mind was far from dresses. What was it that his lordship feared might happen? Something that caused him to spend the nights in the adjoining room.

Faith had watched the food and water carefully and the Countess remained bright and alert. Perhaps, she thought, she had alarmed herself unduly.

She found her mind often occupied with the problem of the secret passageway. She had promised his lordship that she would not chase ghosts. She had not promised him that she would not look for the passageway.

And so, on the third afternoon of sewing, when she finished the green gown, she turned to the Countess. "Milady, I am dreadfully tired of sewing. If there *were* a secret passageway, would it not lead past this room?"

The Countess nodded. "I suppose. This was the first Earl's room. But I am not interested in such things."

"Please, milady. Do you mind if I look for it? It really ought to open into this room."

The Countess chuckled. "You are wasting your time, child, but I suppose that sewing is dull work for you. Do what you please in here, but do not go searching about in other parts of the castle. You are too valuable to me."

"Do you really think that I would be in danger?"

The Countess smiled. "Secret passageways are always dangerous. Doors may easily swing shut, locking one inside. Do your exploring here, Faith. It will liven my day, too."

"Thank you, milady. You are most kind."

"Nonsense," grinned the Countess. "I just like a little excitement now and then."

Faith grinned too. Now, she thought to herself, where would one be likely to find the entrance to a secret passageway? Probably not on the wall by the hall. She considered the room.

"Try around the fireplace," suggested the Countess. "Seems to me Henry used to tell tales about such things being around fireplaces."

"Yes, milady." Faith felt a rising excitement as she approached the fireplace.

"Usually one knocks on the wall or the paneling," explained the Countess, "and listens for a difference in the sound."

Obediently Faith began to knock with

her knuckles on the wood paneling that surrounded the huge old fireplace. She knocked till her knuckles were sore, but with no result. Finally she stopped and sighed, rubbing her bruised hands.

"It's no use, child," called the Countess from the great bed. "Such things are not meant to be easily found."

"Yes, I know. But if there are passageways, and his lordship says the story is true, then there must be a way into this room."

"Indeed," replied the Countess. "But that doesn't mean that it must be found."

Faith smiled. "I am a most persistent person, milady. The panels in the wall all sound the same. Therefore the passageway entrance cannot be there. Now, where else could it be?"

Hands on hips, she turned to face the fireplace. She *would* find the passageway entrance. She simply would.

Purposefully she approached the massive old fireplace. Surely no passageway entrance could exist there. And yet she continued to run her fingers over the rough-hewn stone.

Perhaps on the hearth, or up inside the chimney, she thought, leaning over to look up. But there seemed to be nothing there. Heaving a sigh, Faith began to move away. There was the sound of tearing cloth.

Turning, she discovered that she had caught her gown on a nail that was sticking out of the mortar.

Faith disengaged her dress and again moved away. The builder should have been more careful. The fireplace was hardly the place for a nail.

A nail! Faith stopped suddenly. With a little squeal of delight she knelt to examine the offending nail. It was long and thick, probably not a nail at all but a thin metal rod. Gingerly Faith moved the rod, first right, then left, then up, then down. There was the smallest of sounds and one side of the fireplace silently pivoted out. In the opening behind it Faith saw the darkness of a passageway.

"By all that's holy!" breathed the Countess from the big bed. "Henry was right. Faith, you found it!"

"Yes, milady, I did."

Faith reached for the tinder and flint and lit a candle.

"What are you doing?" the Countess demanded.

"I am going to explore the passageway. I want to see where it goes."

"Faith!"

"Come, milady. I'll be safe enough. No ghosts are abroad in daylight. I shall leave it open and you ring for Deevers. That way you'll have company while I'm gone."

"I don't like it," said the Countess. "I don't like it at all."

"Ring for Deevers," repeated Faith as she picked up the candle and stepped into the darkness.

The passageway smelled old and musty and Faith moved along carefully, shielding the candle as she went. Her heart was pounding in her throat, but she would not turn back.

Softly she stepped along the passageway. It was remarkably free of cobwebs, she thought, and then the realization struck her. No spider webs or cobwebs festooned this passage for one reason – someone had been using it regularly!

The thought sent a shiver racing over her, but still she refused to retrace her steps. And then in the darkness to one side of her appeared a faint line of light. It seemed to be coming from something on the wall. Faith stepped closer to investigate and discovered that the line of light was in reality an opening into a room. She put her eyes to the crack and held back a cry. She was looking down into her own room!

Carefully she examined the wall, but there did not seem to be any entrance to her room. She breathed a sigh of relief. Anyone coming on her unawares would have to come through the Countess's room. But they *could* watch her. They *had* watched her, she realized, recalling several occasions when she had wondered at a strange prickling sensation on the back of her neck.

But who could have been using the passageway and for what purpose? She could hardly suspect the kind and mild Mr. Felix. He was such a perfect gentleman. Lady Clarisse might well do anything to get the money, but now, at least, she stood to gain nothing from the Countess's death. And that left the Earl. Faith's heart seemed to be pounding in her throat. The Earl was the only one with anything to gain. She could see that. But she could also see that he loved his aunt.

Surely such feelings could not be faked. And what of her own feelings of peace and security, the feelings that his lordship somehow inspired in her? She sighed. It was too much of a puzzle. She would just explore this passageway and return to the Countess. All this speculation was worthless.

As quietly as possible Faith proceeded in the darkness. She passed by the next line of light without looking. Undoubtedly that would be the room next to hers, the room that the Earl now occupied. But after that, every time she noticed a peephole she stopped and surveyed the room. One room she recognized from its array of cosmetics and perfumes as that of Lady Clarisse. Another was Mr. Felix's and she moved swiftly away from that. It seemed almost rude to be gazing into a person's private domain.

But at one place, when she spied a coat of blue superfine and a pair of well-polished boots that she recognized immediately as belonging to the Earl, she stood gazing for long minutes. So this was the room he ordinarily used. It was a strangely austere room for a man of the Earl's position and Faith could only assume that it was so by his orders. For all the others' rooms seemed much more opulent.

Finally Faith forced herself to move on. How strange that just looking at his room should give her again that feeling of safety.

As she continued to creep along the passageway, sheltering her candle, she realized that the floor beneath her feet was sloping downhill. There were no more peepholes and the passageway became narrow and tunnel-like.

Faith followed it for what seemed like a long way, twisting and turning. Then suddenly, the light of the flickering candle revealed a small door. It seemed to be set in rock

172

and she, not daring to put the candle down, decided not to touch it.

There were cobwebs across it, Faith realized suddenly, a great many cobwebs, which meant that no one had come in or out of that door for a long time. Of course, there might well be another exit at the other end of the passageway, so she could not say for sure that whoever was using the passageway was someone within the castle.

Faith felt herself growing chill. It was time to get back to the Countess. She had been gone quite some time.

The way back seemed very long and more than once Faith stopped, listening for the sound of footsteps in the shadows behind her. When she finally reached the entrance to the Countess's room, she knew that she had explored enough for one day. The other part of the passageway extended into the darkness. She shivered. Whatever lay there must be discovered another day. This had been quite enough.

She stepped softly into the room and was greeted by the Countess's sigh of relief. "My word, girl, but you've given me a scare. You were gone simply ages. Come here quick and tell me about it. But first close that thing up. I keep expecting someone to jump out of it."

Faith put down the candle and moved the

lever. Soundlessly the fireplace swung to.

"Where is Deevers?" asked Faith, suddenly aware that the old servant was not present.

The Countess smiled. "Deevers is an old friend and a trusted one. But she has a timid nature. Such a revelation would frighten the poor woman half to death. Come, tell me."

Faith settled on a chair beside the bed. "It goes past many rooms. I only followed it one way. There are peepholes to look into the rooms."

The Countess shook her head. "And to think that I used to scoff at Henry when he told me tales of such things. Do go on."

"The passageway slants down hill and becomes almost a tunnel. And it ends at a door," said Faith. "A door set in rock."

The Countess nodded. "I expect that door leads out into the moors. You didn't open it?"

Faith shook her head. "No, milady. It hadn't been opened for some time. It was covered with dust and cobwebs." Faith paused.

"Go on," commanded the Countess. "I see by your face that there's more."

"The passageway itself – and the peepholes – all were free of cobwebs. Someone has been using the passageway frequently." Faith shivered again at the thought of unknown eyes spying on her.

"I see," said the Countess calmly.

Faith could not help marveling at the old woman's behavior. After all, she was helpless in the big bed and she had just discovered that someone was spying on her and had access to her room. And yet there she lay, talking of the whole thing in quite even tones.

Faith smiled. "Goodness, milady, you are very brave."

The Countess shook her head. "Nonsense, girl. I told you. I'm not afraid of dying. I expect to see my Henry then. And anyway, anyone who wanted to dispose of me could have done it long ago. No, I believe I am safe enough, for the present, at least. But you did give me a turn when you were gone so long."

"I'm sorry, milady, but I wanted to see where it went."

The Countess nodded. "Of course you did. But now I am excessively weary and must rest awhile." She grinned. "So much excitement is bad for my old bones."

Faith rearranged the pillows and helped the Countess get comfortable. Then she settled herself in a nearby chair. There was a deal of thinking to be done before dinner.

A frown creased her forehead as she tried to decide what was the proper thing to do. Should she tell the Earl of her discovery? If he were not the person who had been creeping about, then he should know. But, if he were that person . . .

Faith found herself holding her breath. Two warnings she had had about the Earl. Lady Clarisse's, prompted as it was by obvious jealousy, could be safely ignored. But what of Mr. Felix's suspicions of his brother? Should she ignore those?

Faith's heart pounded again as she remembered the Earl's lips on hers, his arms encircling her, the tender way he had brushed back the hair on her forehead the night before. Surely such a man could not have intentions on his aunt's life? Surely all her feelings about him could not be wrong?

Suddenly Faith's memory presented her with a picture of the scene on the rocks. For a moment, as she saw his lordship's hand outstretched toward her, she had experienced sheer panic. But he had not pushed her; he had pulled her toward him. But if she had not turned when she did, if she had remained with her back to him, contemplating that beauty, would he have pushed her then?

A cold shiver ran through her. Life had become very complicated lately, she thought with a sigh. The old ways that had always proved so useful in dealing with life no longer seemed applicable. She was thrust into a strange new world, a world with different rules that she might not even know, let alone understand.

Now, if it had been a question simply of her own safety, she would have trusted the Earl, trusted him implicitly. But it was not her life that was in jeopardy. The Countess's health and safety were *her* responsibility. And in such a case she could ill afford to depend merely on her feelings. And yet – she seemed to have nothing more to go on.

If she told the Earl and if he were the guilty one, then she would be even more at his mercy. But if she did not tell him and something happened to the Countess, then it would be her fault.

Faith sighed again and finally made her decision. The Countess trusted his lordship and, in some strange way, she herself wanted to trust him. She would tell him – simply tell him.

But then a new problem presented itself. How was she to tell him when at any time someone might be spying on them from the passageway?

Sometime later, washed and clad in the new green gown, Faith descended the broad staircase. She had debated about wearing the new gown, but, since it was done and since his lordship had been so vehement about getting rid of the old ones, she had thought it advisable to wear it. Besides, she admitted to herself that she had wanted to see the look in his eyes when she appeared. She knew, of course, that it was sheer foolishness to even recognize her partiality for the Earl. And surely nothing was going to come of it.

She was not stupid enough to believe that it would. But she could not really help it if she enjoyed the look of admiration in his eyes or that strange smile he sometimes gave her. She was not, of course, ever going to give in to him. Not ever. That was a thought that she kept foremost in her mind. Absolutely never.

Faith looked toward the library. She had come down early in the hope of seeing his lordship alone. She approached the library door and peered in. He was standing with his back to the door, very still, as though deep in thought. "Milord," she faltered.

He swung around. "Yes? Oh, Miss Duncan." His eyes slid over the dress but he made no comment.

She was conscious of a sense of disappointment because he had not used her Christian name. The sound of it on his lips gave her a strange sense of joy.

"I – milord, I need to speak to you – privately."

The Earl looked around. "We are alone."

"I – I would like a breath of fresh air. Would you step out with me for a moment?"

"Of course. Shall we go now?"

Faith nodded and put her hand on the arm he extended. They paused momentarily in the great hall where his lordship picked up his cloak. "The sun is still up, but the wind is chill. We'll just take my cloak so you needn't go up after yours."

Faith nodded.

Outside the great door the Earl put the cloak around her shoulders. She was conscious of the odor of horses and heather, a strangely pleasant smell. "Thank you," she murmured.

The Earl moved off, away from the castle, and stopped. "I take it that you feared we would be overheard."

Faith nodded. Now that the time to tell him had arrived she was nervous about it. And yet she must tell him. She could not face this alone. "The passageway," she faltered, "it opens into the Countess's room. I – I found the lever that opens it."

"I see." The Earl's dark eyes were opaque. She could read no emotion there. "Did you look into it?"

Faith nodded. "Yes, milord."

"And did you go all the way to the door?" he asked evenly.

"You knew! You knew about it all along." Her heart pounded in her throat.

His lordship nodded. "I found it when I was just a lad. I was very persistent then." His eyes gleamed. "Still am."

"Someone has been using it," Faith cried. "Did you know that?"

The Earl nodded. "Yes, I knew. But it was not I. At least, not I alone. The day you thought Aunt had been drugged, I looked into the passageway. I realized then that someone was using it. I have tried to discover who it is. But I have been unsuccessful." He smiled ruefully. "The 'ghost' – or whatever – persists in eluding me."

Faith shivered. A chill wind was penetrating the cloak. "I do not understand any of this," she faltered.

The Earl reached out and put an arm around her shivering shoulders. "Nor do I. At least not at this point. But I shall. Believe me, I shall." He pulled her against his side. "In the meantime, do not do foolhardy things."

Faith nodded, but she made no verbal promises. She must keep the right to act as she thought best. A sudden fit of shivering attacked her. How she longed to trust this man completely and absolutely – and she dared not. She simply dared not.

The shivering increased until her teeth began to chatter.

The Earl looked at her with concern and then he pulled her into his arms. It was warm there and she felt a great sense of peace stealing over her. She felt his lips brush her hair and then his voice came to her ears. Deep and low, it seemed to vibrate in her very bones. "I have been waiting," he said softly. "I have never waited so long for a woman. Never."

"Milord," murmured Faith against his shoulder. "You must not say such things. You know I cannot do what you ask."

"Why not?" His lips moved along the top of her ear, causing strange sensations in her body.

"You – you know. I must have a care for my reputation. My good name."

"No one will ever know," he whispered, his lips continuing their journey to where the pulse pounded in her throat.

Faith moaned. "I should know. Milord, please!"

And then his lips sought and found hers, found them in a kiss that left her clinging to him weakly.

"Tonight –" he began.

Faith, fighting to regain her sanity, tore herself from his arms. She was breathing

181

heavily and she strove to control her trembling. "You forget yourself, milord. I am an honorable woman. I cannot accede to such a proposal."

Amusement glinted in the Earl's dark eyes. "Very well, I shall not push you further. But be advised, I am still waiting." With that he drew her arm through his and returned to the castle.

As they entered the great hall they were met by Lady Clarisse and Mr. Felix. The lady's gray eyes were icy and Mr. Felix's seemed sad. What was she doing with his rakish brother, they seemed to ask her? And Faith, feeling herself color up, had no good answer.

The Earl met Lady Clarisse's freezing eyes. "Miss Duncan and I were speaking of Aunt's health. And since she gets so little fresh air I suggested a walk outside."

Lady Clarisse's expression softened as she turned to the Earl. "You are always so considerate, Hugh, my dear."

His lordship merely shrugged.

"Miss Duncan," said Mr. Felix, his eyes still saddened by some unspoken accusation. "I hope that my aunt has not suffered a relapse."

"Oh no, sir." Faith hastened to assure him. "Your aunt is making good progress. Soon, perhaps tomorrow, we expect to move her into a chair for a while."

"Oh," cried Mr Felix. "What excellent news. We should all have a glass of wine to celebrate."

He extended his arm to Faith. Suddenly she was conscious of the Earl's cloak and her fingers flew to her throat.

"Allow me." Urbanely the Earl undid the strings.

"Thank you," murmured Faith and then she took the arm that Mr. Felix offered. How strange, she thought to herself, that when his lordship took away his cloak a certain sense of safety went with it.

Chapter 12

Day followed day. Autumn came to Yorkshire and, though there were few trees to lose their leaves, the green of the moors began to turn brown, and the heather faded to a dusty purple.

Faith, stitching on her new dresses, kept close watch on the Countess. Very slowly the old woman was regaining her strength. And slowly Faith began to relax a little. Nothing more had happened. Perhaps it had all been a mistake. Perhaps no one had meant the Countess any harm.

And then it was time for the full moon again. Faith would not, perhaps, have realized it, if Mr. Felix hadn't mentioned the fact at dinner. "It's the full moon again tonight," he said with his gentle smile. "I wonder if the ghost will walk."

Lady Clarisse shivered dramatically and leaned toward the Earl. "If she does," said that gentleman languidly, "I suggest we all stay in our warm beds." His glance flicked briefly over Faith as he said this and she realized that it was meant to reinforce his previous orders. She was also well aware that his lordship had not for some time spent the nights in his own bed. He had continued his vigil in the room next to hers, a vigil that gave her a great feeling of safety.

Later, after readying the Countess for the night, Faith sank into a chair by the fireplace to think. She sat there for some time, chasing certain thoughts around and around and arriving nowhere. Would the ghost walk, she wondered. And was it a ghost? Or was it someone from the castle? But, as usual, there were no answers to her questions and finally her head began to nod.

She was sinking into a sort of a doze when a

small scraping sound made her sit erect. The fireplace was just closing. Someone had been in the room! That was Faith's first thought as she leaped to her feet. Suddenly the frustration of all the days of worry and waiting seemed to burst upon her. Whoever was doing this must be discovered and stopped. A quick look told Faith that the Countess was sleeping peacefully. Without thinking any further, she pressed the lever that opened the door and set off in the direction she had taken before.

The passageway was dark and gloomy but ahead she saw an occasional flicker of light in the shadows. Faith hurried along, guiding herself by a hand on the wall, trying to move quietly but determined to catch up with the person ahead of her.

Under her feet the passageway began to slope downhill. Either the person would have to leave the tunnel through one of the entrances to the rooms or go all the way to the door. In either case she should be able to catch up. The determination to end her uncertainty was so strong that she did not consider what she would do when she reached the intruder.

And then, as she rounded a corner in the tunnel, something heavy fell over her head. She was muffled in the folds of something like a cloak.

Faith tried to fight her way free, but

strong arms were around her, keeping her hands pinned at her sides. Then she was being dragged down the passageway by her assailant. She struggled, but the cloak's heavy folds cut off her air. She felt lightheaded and dizzy, and her heart pounded in her throat. Who could it be that held her so tightly in his grasp? The faint smell of horses and heather came to her nostrils. It seemed to be coming from the cloak that muffled her head.

Faith shuddered and felt her knees go weak. It was that very smell – the smell of heather and horses – that she had noticed when his lordship had put his cloak around her on the day she told him about finding the passageway. Dear God, was it the Earl who was dragging her, half-unconscious, down the tunnel?

Faith tried to muster some strength, but the thought that it might be the Earl whose hands held her so cruelly seemed to drain away her remaining strength. She was not getting much air and it was difficult to breathe.

Suddenly Faith realized that her assailant had stopped. She renewed her struggles to escape the folds of the cloak, but just as she thought she might get her head free, her hands were jerked behind her and a loop of rope circled her wrists.

It couldn't be the Earl, Faith told herself,

as the darkness came up to claim her. She couldn't have been mistaken in her trust in him.

When Faith came back to consciousness, she grew aware of a strange, rocking motion. For a moment she could not recall why it was so difficult to breathe and move. Then realization came back to her. She had been captured by someone in the passageway and now, now she decided, she was on horseback. Terror struck deep into her heart. Where was he taking her, this faceless man? It must be a man who held her with an iron arm.

She did not begin struggling again. It was of little use.

It seemed to Faith that they rode for a long time, but she had no way of measuring, and then suddenly the horse stopped. The arm that held her loosened as the man dismounted. Then he pulled her roughly from the horse's back and set her on her feet. It was impossible for her to keep her balance and she sank to her knees.

She heard a strange laugh, harsh and brutal, rather like the Earl's laughter. But the heavy folds of the cloak distorted all sound. She felt the loop on her wrists being loosened and then in a moment there was the rhythmic sound of hooves fading into the distance.

Faith fought the cloak and finally succeeded

in extricating herself from its folds, but by that time the retreating figure was a mere speck in the distance – an erect figure on a dark horse.

Faith shivered and looked around her. The night air was quite chill and without thinking she stooped for the cloak and flung it around her shoulders. The scent of horses and heather came faintly to her nostrils and the tears rose unbidden to her eyes. This *was* the Earl's cloak. She recognized it in the moonlight.

But, said a small voice in her head, that did not mean that the Earl had done this to her. She looked around. The moon was full and shone on the rolling hills and waves of dried heather that stretched in every direction. She was alone somewhere on the moors and she had no idea in which direction the castle lay, no idea how soon anyone might miss her.

Faith sank down onto a large tuft of grass. It was foolishness of the worst sort to try to find the castle in the darkness. One false step and she might be helplessly mired.

She shivered uncontrollably as she considered her situation. The Earl had warned her of the dangers of the moor. She dared not move from where the man had left her. Not when the moon might at any moment go behind a cloud and leave her in utter darkness.

She wrapped the cloak more tightly around her. The sensible thing seemed to be to wait – right where she was – until someone found her. Surely when the Earl discovered her gone, he would look for her. And he knew the moors well.

But, what if the horseman who had brought her here were the Earl himself? Then no help would be forthcoming. No help at all. For if the Earl had done this to her, then it had been he and he alone doing the spying, and he meant for her to die here. He must know that with the warning he had given her she would be too frightened to try to find her way alone.

Faith bit her bottom lip. How was she to tell what to do? If she chose wrong, she might very well die here on the moor, if not from falling into a bog hole, then from exposure.

And all she had to help her in her choice were feelings – feelings about Mr. Felix, feelings about his lordship, feelings about Lady Clarisse. It seemed unlikely that Lady Clarisse was involved in this. Not because of her fine character, thought Faith with a bitter smile, but because it had definitely been a man who had captured her – a hard man, lean and strong. Like the Earl, she thought with a little sob.

Certainly the man could not have been Mr. Felix. He would not handle a woman so roughly. That brought her again to the Earl – a man that she trusted in spite of herself. Even now, she realized, the knowledge that it was *his* cloak around her was comforting. Was she such a fool, had she been so thoroughly deceived by the man, that she could persist in trusting him when he sought to kill her?

With a sigh Faith rubbed her chilled hands together. The Countess trusted his lordship and refused to hear ill of him. But she, too, loved him.

Suddenly Faith realized the import of her thoughts. It was true. She *did* love the Earl. It was unfortunate, of course, for the only way to consummate their love was dishonorable.

And then she began to laugh; bitterly, almost hysterically, she laughed until her laughter turned to tears. Alone, in the middle of the night, on the Yorkshire moors, with no way to reach the safety of the castle, and she was thinking that her love made her vulnerable to dishonor. The tears slid faster down her cheeks. What was far more likely was that it made her vulnerable – to death!

For long moments Faith let the tears come. Certainly no one could see them here. Finally she dried her eyes on the edge of the cloak.

190

There was no point in giving way to hysteria. The sensible thing to do now was to sleep. In the morning she would consider the alternatives again. She would be calmer then, able to think more clearly.

Carefully Faith got to her feet and looked at the ground around her. She was on the crest of a swelling slope. The ground had not seemed damp. But still, as she moved, she put her weight tentatively on each foot, ready to throw herself backward to safety. But the little hill seemed safe enough.

She gathered an armful of dried heather and made herself a couch. Lying down she would be out of the wind. Then, wrapping the cloak around her, she lay down and tried to rest.

Sleep was long in coming. Her mind was a chaos of thoughts. Scenes seemed to flash on her closed eyelids. The interview with Mr. Felix. How long ago *that* seemed. Her first meeting with the Earl. That kiss and subsequent ones. Her lips seemed almost to feel the touch of his.

Faith's lower lip quivered. If only he were here to take her in his arms and comfort her, and then lead her to safety. If only she had listened to his warnings, sane and sensible warnings, she would not be here, alone and hurting. It was obvious that her assailant had done this thing to her because he was afraid she would recognize him.

She shivered again, clasping her arms about herself under the cloak. The night was chill and the wind seemed to cut through to her bones. Once she stumbled to her feet to gather more heather and piled it around her as a windbreak.

Finally, exhausted and still shivering, she fell asleep. But even in slumber her frantic mind gave her no rest. She was haunted by his lordship's mocking smiles. In her dreams he opened his arms to her and when she rushed into their safety, she would find that he had turned into the faceless man who had left her alone on the moors.

In one of her dreams she was fleeing that man and fell into a bog hole. The slimy wet soil seemed to pull her down into its depths. She felt the chill, dank water closing over her head. Her mouth and nose filled with it.

She woke screaming and discovered that while she slept day had come and with it a driving, chilling rain. It was that rain, falling on her face while she slept, that had induced her nightmare.

Faith sat up stiffly. She was terribly cold. Her hair was a sodden mass against her neck and the cloak was almost soaked through. She must get to her feet, she thought, her mind still benumbed by sleep. She must get to her feet and walk to keep warm.

Slowly she forced herself to rise. The cloak was damp, but still she clung to it. It helped somewhat in keeping off the wind. And it was his. That thought would not leave her mind. She clung to it numbly.

For a moment she stared around her. Here on the heath there was no place to take shelter. Not a tree, not even a rock. Nothing but heather, all as soaked as she, as far as the eye could see.

Well, she thought to herself, pushing back the tendrils of wet hair that lay against her cheeks, she must walk to restore the circulation to her chilled limbs. And she dared not venture off this little slope. To do that if the sun were shining would be dangerous. To do it now would be to invite almost certain death.

She hugged the sodden cloak around her and began to pace. Ten steps forward, ten steps back. Ten steps forward, ten steps back. Her thin house shoes, already sodden, squished in the wet heather with every step. Her feet were wet and cold. There was, she suspected, not a dry spot anywhere on her numbed, stiff body.

The rain dripped from her hair and ran down her face onto the cloak. After a time it mixed indiscriminately with the tears that fell from her eyes. "He will come. He will come," she told herself repeatedly. It became a litany that accompanied each step. "He will come. The Earl will come."

And then she turned and began the whole litany again.

She had no idea how long she had paced, dragging one foot after the other, when she fell. The longing was great upon her simply to lie there in the mud and let unconsciousness claim her. The Earl had not come. Perhaps it had been he who had left her here – to die.

But something within her refused to give up. She would not simply lie down and die. No, she would keep moving, keep herself warm, and help would come. The Countess would miss her. The Countess would insist that they find her.

Faith clung to this hope as she forced herself up, to keep pacing the path that she had worn through the wet and muddy heather. Someone would come.

Finally there came a time when she fell and could not rise again. She tried to muster whatever strength she had left, but there was nothing. For all her efforts she remained lying, her face against the wet heather, a huddled heap under the great cloak.

It was no use, she told herself. Perhaps it had been the Earl who had left her there so cruelly, perhaps it had been someone else. But it was unlikely she was ever to know, she thought, as the numbing weariness stole over her. She was unlikely to know anything again. And whispering his name she gave herself up to the warm darkness.

Faith moaned softly as she heard someone calling her. He seemed far away; his voice came to her as over a great distance. "Faith! Faith! Speak to me."

She was warm and comfortable and he was far away. And somehow she knew that to answer that summons was to go back to a world of cold and misery.

But the voice was insistent. "Faith! Wake up! You must wake up!"

She felt hands on her shoulders, shaking her roughly, and she managed to open her eyes. It was the Earl, bending over her. He dragged her roughly to her feet and shook her again. "Faith! You must wake up. Speak to me."

Her lips formed his name, but she could not speak it. And her legs refused to support her weight. She stared at him from unbelieving eyes. All of this was a dream, of course. Any minute now he would turn into someone else,

195

someone terrifying, like the unknown man who had left her here to die.

"Crazy little fool." He shook her, in exasperation, it seemed. "I told you to stay put. Not to go off exploring."

As her eyelids began to close, he shook her again. And she was glad. For this must be real, not a dream as she had thought. He didn't turn into someone else. He was solidly, substantially there.

"Hugh," she said, this time getting the word out, and trying to smile.

The Earl continued to frown as he swung her up in his arms. "Stupid little fool. You're lucky to be alive."

"Didn't move," muttered Faith against his sodden chest. "Knew you'd find me." She closed her eyes peacefully and so did not see the strange look that crossed his lordship's features at this piece of information.

He set her on the back of the patiently waiting horse and swung up behind her. As his arm went around her and he pulled her close against him, Faith sighed in contentment. It didn't matter that she was cold and wet and weary to the bone – or even that something in her chest made it hurt to breathe. He *had* come. Her trust in him had not been misplaced. He had come and he had saved her. There was nothing more to worry about. Except – "The Countess?" she mumbled.

"Aunt is all right," he said gruffly. "But no thanks to you, running off like that." But by that time Faith had already slipped back into the welcoming darkness and heard no more.

Chapter 13

Faith stirred in the bed. There was something sitting on her chest, she thought hazily, something big that made it hard to breathe. Like the time that Mrs. Petrie's cat had decided to sleep on her and she had wakened to find a pair of green feline eyes staring into hers. But she had seen no cats at Moorshead.

Carefully she raised her eyelids. They seemed exceedingly heavy but she did manage to open them. And then she started in surprise. The sun was streaming into the room. She should have been up and about long ago, tending to the Countess. She made a movement to throw back the covers and realized with a shock that she was too weak to raise them. And then as she remembered it all a moan escaped her. She must have been ill.

The sound brought his lordship to the side

of the bed. There was something different about him, she thought. His face was haggard and a dark stubble of beard clothed his cheeks.

Her lips formed his Christian name, but she remembered her place in time. "Milord?"

"You have been ill," he said gruffly. "You took a chill."

Under the heavy covers Faith shivered. His lordship brushed a strand of hair from her forehead. "You have been very ill, but you are better now."

"The Countess?"

"Aunt is well. We have been concerned over *you*."

"I must be about my duties," Faith began, trying to rise.

The Earl pushed her back against the pillows. It took very little effort for him to keep her there. She was far too weak to fight him. "Can you tell me what happened?" he asked, his dark eyes searching hers. There was something strange in the way he looked at her, but she could not quite tell what it was.

"Yes. I was dozing in the chair while the Countess slept. And I heard the fireplace door closing. The sound woke me." She took a deep breath. Those dark eyes so close to her own were gazing at her accusingly, she thought. "I – I followed. I had to see who it was."

"And did you see?"

Faith shook her head. "No. I thought to catch him at the door, but before I reached it someone threw a cloak over my head." She swallowed hastily as the terror returned to engulf her. "He – he tied my hands and put me on the horse before him."

"And left you on the moor."

She nodded

"Did you see him at all? Anything that would help?"

Faith shook her head. "I didn't see anything. I was muffled in the cloak. But it was a man and he was lean and hard – like you." She faltered, but refused to drop her eyes.

"I see. And it was my cloak that he wrapped you in, was it not?"

Faith nodded. She dared not say anymore. Would he ask her if she had suspected him? And if he did, what would she answer?

"When I found you," he remarked dryly, "you said that you had expected me to come for you."

Faith felt the color rush to her face. "I – I expected that the Countess would find me gone and ask you to hunt for me."

"And how did you know that I would look

for you on the moors?" he asked, his eyes boring into hers.

She shook her head. "I don't know. I felt – somehow – that you would know where to find me." She tried to tear her eyes away from him, afraid of what they would reveal.

"Why didn't you try to find your way back to the castle?"

"You told me, you warned me about the dangers."

"And so you stayed put, trusting me to find you."

Faith nodded. Vaguely she could remember some delirious dreams in which she had babbled her assurance that he would find her. She seemed to recall having repeated his name over and over, like a spell to keep away evil.

"Do you not think it was rather unwise to put your trust in a man of my loose reputation?" he asked gravely.

Faith colored again. "A man may be many things," she replied. "One need not necessarily preclude another." She smiled. "And my trust was not misplaced, was it?"

The Earl smiled, a strange smile with a touch of tenderness in it. "No," he replied. "*This* time it was not misplaced."

She wondered momentarily at that curious

emphasis on the word *this,* but he made no more comment.

"Tell me," she said. "How *did* you know where to look for me?"

That strange smile crossed his face again. "When I came to see if you were safe for the night, you did not answer my knock. I found your room empty, Aunt asleep, and the passageway door open. I called Deevers to sit with Aunt, got my pistol and followed. But I was too late. I saw that the door in the rock – the one that leads onto the moors – had been opened. And, since I did not find you, I suspected the worst."

Faith shivered. If he had not found her, by now she would be dead from the cold and wet.

The Earl continued. "When I prepared to set out after you, I found that my cloak was missing."

"What time of day did you find me?" asked Faith, shivering again as she recalled her weary efforts to keep warm.

"It was late afternoon," said the Earl. "The moors are wide and difficult to ride. And the rain made matters worse."

"I am very glad you came after me." Faith was aware of how ineffectual her words were.

"I did not intend to return until I had found you," he said curtly, his mouth settling into a grim line. "And I will deal harshly with him when I find the person who did this."

"I do not understand why anyone should want to harm me," said Faith.

"Quite likely they should not have, had you not attempted to follow them. Didn't I tell you to stay put?"

Faith nodded.

"But – but I forgot. I wanted to see who it was."

"And what did you intend to do then?" he asked in deceptively soft tones.

"I – I didn't think that far."

"Precisely," said his lordship in a voice that made her quiver. "You – did not think – at all. I suggest that in the future you try thinking."

Faith felt herself clutching at the covers. Why should his anger make her feel so weak and vulnerable?

"I – I'm sorry," she stammered. No more words would come and she felt like a very bad, very little girl.

His lordship's face lightened. "You will not disobey me in these matters again?"

"No, milord," she managed.

"No, Hugh," he said.

Faith swallowed. He reached for one of her hands that clutched nervously at the covers and took it gently in his own. "Say it," he repeated.

"But, milord," Faith protested. "That – that is improper."

"Such things are immaterial to me," his lordship insisted. "I wish to hear you speak my Christian name again."

"Again?" Faith tried to withdraw her fingers from his, but he kept them firmly captive.

"Yes. You were very ill. Delirious, with a fever. And you often spoke my name."

"Your Christian name?" asked Faith, conscious that her lower lip had begun to quiver.

His lordship patted the hand that trembled in his own. "My Christian name."

"I am sorry, milord. It was very wrong of me."

"I think not," replied his lordship with that strange smile.

Vaguely Faith could remember those other babblings. Could she have voiced her love for him? She searched his face, but he returned her look quite steadily. "Did I – did I say anything else?"

His dark eyes glanced at her. "A few babblings. Nothing of any import."

"Nothing?" she repeated.

"Nothing." The Earl's tone was final and she dared not press him any further.

He stroked the hand that he held in his

own. "Do not concern yourself about such things. Now you must rest and regain your strength. Aunt waits impatiently for your return to health."

"Yes, milord."

He reached to arrange the pillows behind her and as he did so he leaned disturbingly close. She clutched the covers to prevent herself from reaching up for him. And then he was leaning over her, the stubble of his beard brushing her cheek as he kissed her forehead. And then his lips were by her ear. "Say it, say my name," he whispered.

"Hugh." Her lips formed the now familiar word. "Hugh."

His mouth touched her ear and moved down her throat to where the pulse pounded. "My love," he whispered. And then he was on his feet, those dark eyes laughing at her. He rubbed the black stubble ruefully. "And now I believe I had best go remove this from my chin. Few women have seen me in this condition. Two days' stubble on my chin. Two days in the same clothes." He shook his head. "My reputation will be quite ruined if the word gets out."

"I shall tell no one. You may be sure of that," replied Faith with a smile. "But two days, milord? What could have caused you to forgo your toilet for two days?"

The Earl smiled laconically. "You," he replied, and, turning on his heel, he strode off.

He was gone before the full realization came to her. She had been ill for two days and he had spent those two days by her side. He had not even left her to be shaved or to put on fresh clothes.

A warm feeling of satisfaction spread over her; it seemed to give her new strength. Again those whispered words echoed in her ear. "My love," he had said. "My love."

They were simple words, words that men often spoke without thinking, without really meaning. She knew that, Faith told herself. She knew it quite well. And yet those words seemed to function for her as his cloak had. They gave her protection and a feeling of safety. And with that thought she closed her eyes and drifted back to sleep.

When Faith woke again, the Earl had returned. The dark circles were still there under his eyes. But the dark stubble was gone and he had bathed and put on fresh clothes. His shoulders were as erect as ever and his dark eyes seemed to envelop her.

"Milord."

"You see me refreshed, a new man," he said with a wry smile. "It's miraculous what a shave and a bath and clean clothes can do for a man."

Privately Faith thought that he had never appeared more handsome to her than when in his disheveled state he had told her that he had spent two days and nights in vigil by her bed.

She smiled at him and said nothing.

His lordship returned the smile and there was mischief in his eyes. "I have come on an errand from Aunt," he said.

"Yes, milord?"

"She insists that she must see with her own eyes that you are recovering."

"Of course, milord." She reached for the covers.

"No." His tone was firm but not loud. "You are far too weak for walking." He advanced purposively toward the bed.

"Milord!" Faith protested, but he kept coming.

"There is little point in your protesting," said his lordship. "I have seen your nightdress before. In fact, I have put it on you."

"What!" Faith's hands rose to cover her scarlet cheeks.

"There is little cause for alarm," the Earl commented dryly. "I have seen many female bodies. Yours was no novelty."

"But Deevers? The maids?"

The Earl shrugged. "Deevers was busy with Aunt and the maids are all unreliable gigglers. You were quite ill. I could not trust you to such ineffectual hands."

"But oh –" Faith could find no words to voice her consternation. He had looked on her –

"Do not be such a prude," he exclaimed. "Even if you are the virgin innocent you claim to be, I did you no harm." His eyes flashed at her. "I have done somewhat more in my four and thirty years than build a reputation as a rake. I served with Nelson at Trafalgar when I was young and there I learned a great deal about caring for the ill. Here, that night, I was the only trustworthy one with the necessary knowledge. And I used it."

He raised a quizzical eyebrow. "Perhaps you would have preferred that I respect your modesty and let you die."

Faith shivered. "I did not mean to be ungrateful," she stammered.

"Good." The Earl pulled aside the covers. "Now that we have dispensed with false modesty, I intend to carry you in so that Aunt may see you with her own eyes. I trust that you will have no more protests to offer."

Faith managed a small smile. "Whatever you say, milord." She saw the mischief dancing in his eyes and hurried to add,

"That is, I will not protest if you wish to carry me into your aunt's room."

"Very well." His lordship wasted no more words, but bent and slid an arm under her.

Faith's arms went up to curl around his neck and she leaned her head against his shoulder. It was very good to be in his arms. She sighed in great contentment.

He pulled a cover from the bed and wrapped it over her. "Now, you will be warm."

"Yes, Hugh." the words escaped her before she thought, but his lordship merely smiled and strode across to the door that led into the Countess's room.

He carried her up to the great bed and set her upon a chair that had been drawn up beside it. Carefully he tucked the cover around her. "Here she is," he said. "Alive and well. A little weak perhaps. But a few days' rest will cure that. I daresay that next week we'll find her back on her feet bullying you into eating properly."

The Countess chuckled but her bright eyes inspected Faith carefully. "Are you sure, Hugh? She looks excessively pale."

"She *is* excessively pale," said his lordship cheerfully. "But that is normal. She has been through a harrowing experience and has been quite ill. But there is no need for alarm."

208

The Countess spoke to Faith. "My dear girl, how do you feel?"

"I am a trifle weak, milady," replied Faith. "But otherwise I feel well."

"You must not return to your duties until you are quite recovered," said the Countess firmly.

"Indeed," said his lordship crisply. "I shall see to it that she does not."

The Countess nodded. "Yes, Hugh, I count on you. I should be most unhappy to lose Faith. Next to you and Deevers she's the best friend I have."

A lump formed in Faith's throat. "You are most kind, milady."

"Kindness has little to do with it," snorted the Countess. "I am a selfish old woman and I relish my comforts. You are one of them."

Faith said no more, but the unshed tears that glistened in the Countess's eyes had not been lost on her.

"Take her back to her bed, my boy," said the Countess. "And take good care of her."

The Earl grinned at his aunt. "Indeed, Aunt, I shall. I shall take very good care of her."

Faith, once more gathered into his arms, turned to smile at the Countess. "I will be well soon, milady. I promise you. I am strong and I will recover quickly."

The old woman smiled and waved them away. "I do not want to see you again until you are quite recovered."

As the Earl carried her back to her room, Faith found herself wishing that the distance between the rooms was greater. It was excessively pleasant to be held against his chest, cradled like a little child in his powerful arms. If only she could make it last longer.

The Earl laid her gently on her bed. For long, long moments he stood looking down at her, something strange glittering in his dark eyes. Faith found her heart thudding in her throat. Under the folds of her gown she clenched her hands into fists to prevent them from reaching up for him.

This must stop, she told herself crossly. There was no sense in it, no sense at all. A woman in her circumstances had no business letting herself form a partiality for a lord. She should have known better.

But the Earl was a difficult man to resist. She looked up into his dark eyes and her lips quivered. Still he continued to stare at her.

Faith closed her eyes. If he leaned over now and kissed her, she would be unable to utter a single protest. For, whether her eyes reflected it or not, she knew quite well that her body desired it. Her body desired his kiss.

She sensed that he was moving and then she

felt the covers being drawn up over her. His fingers adjusted the covers under her chin. She felt the touch of fingers on her cheek, and, startled, opened her eyes.

He was grinning down at her cheerfully. "Sleep well, little one. And don't worry about Aunt. Deevers will be in attendance."

"Yes, milord. But I will be well soon and able to resume my du —"

His finger settled on her lips and stopped the words. "*I* will make that decision. I and I alone. Now sleep."

Once more his fingers brushed the hair from her forehead and then he was gone. A great sense of peace stole over Faith and she sighed in contentment as sleep came to claim her.

Chapter 14

Faith spent the rest of the week in bed. Several times she tried to get up, to return to her duties, but she was always prevented by the Earl. "You will stay in that bed and rest until I say otherwise," he ordered sternly.

And even the second time, when she had

really thought herself recovered, a dizziness soon convinced her that he was right.

Much of the week she spent sleeping. Her experience on the moors had been exhausting. She could not deny that. And inevitably the strain of living among those she must suspect had taken its toll of her strength.

For several nights she woke repeatedly in a cold sweat, aware that in her dreams she had been lost on the moors. Sometimes she was stumbling through the morning mist, at others through the icy rain. She walked endless miles up and down the undulating slopes, catching her weary feet in heather and deer-sedge, narrowly avoiding the bog holes. Sometimes she even became hopelessly mired and woke with a scream on her lips. Yet, even in the worst of her nightmares, there was always the feeling that his lordship would find her. Find her and save her.

As she grew stronger the Earl permitted her to sit up for a while each day. She would stare into the flames of the fire and wonder vaguely what was to become of her. The wise thing to do was to remove herself from the castle and the vicinity of the Earl. He was far too dangerous a man. It had been bad enough when he had kissed her savagely and brutally, when he had laughed at her claims to innocence. But now, when he did not kiss her at all, when he treated her with such courtesy, such gentleness, even tenderness, it was far worse.

A sensible woman could withstand the advances of an arrogant rake, but how was she to harden her heart to this man who had such a tender touch and who looked at her with such evident concern in his eyes? A man who had nursed her through a bad illness.

In her confinement she had not expected to receive visitors. The Earl had informed her that he had told the others she was ill. That, he said sternly, was all they needed to know.

He, of course, popped in and out continually. To see, he told her with a twinkle in his eyes, that she was obeying orders.

On the fourth day, when sleep had lost its appeal and she sat propped up by pillows and was even allowed a novel, there came a knock on the door that led from the hall.

The little maid that the Earl had told to stay with her jumped up to answer it. "Is Miss Duncan able to receive visitors?" Faith heard Mr. Felix ask.

The maid giggled and moved toward the bed. " 'Tis Mr. Kingston, miss. An' he wants to know if you be receiving visitors."

Faith, attempting a dignified look, recalled that in the presence of the Earl this maid was the most silent of creatures. "Yes, Milly. Tell him to come in."

She resisted the temptation to pat her hair into place. Somehow she did not think that she would make a very good invalid.

"Ah, Miss Duncan." Mr. Felix advanced to the bed and beamed down on her. "My, but you gave us all such a start. Let us hope you'll soon be over the fever."

Faith managed to keep her face impassive. She wondered at the Earl's subterfuge, but his lordship must have his reasons.

"You are still looking a little peaked," said Mr. Felix, patting the hand that lay on the coverlet. "You must recover quickly. We miss your presence at the dinner table."

"I am feeling much better," said Faith. "And will return to my duties soon."

"Of course you will." He took her fingers in his own. Why was it, Faith caught herself wondering, that his touch did not affect her like that of the Earl?

Mr. Felix leaned still closer until his mild, round face was quite near her own. "I have been so concerned, my dear. So very concerned. Why, when Hugh didn't appear for dinner two nights running you can imagine how worried we were."

214

Faith suppressed a smile. Undoubtedly Lady Clarisse had worried, but it had not been about Faith's recovery. "I am sorry to cause you concern, sir. But this illness caught me unawares."

Mr. Felix's hand tightened on hers. "I thought perhaps I might lose you." He swallowed several times as though to overcome some great emotion. "And before I had asked you the question that has been so long on my mind."

Oh dear, Faith thought. He did mean to make her an offer and she did not know what to do about it. Obviously the sensible thing was to accept. Certainly the Earl did not mean to do honorably by her. Earls did not marry nurse-companions.

And soon the Earl would be returning to London. Mr. Felix would give her a home and respect. She need never again worry about her future.

Certainly that was something which must be considered. But she did not believe that the Countess would be at all pleased by such an arrangement. She persisted in mistrusting poor Mr. Felix, though Faith, for the life of her, could not understand why. It was clear to her that Mr. Felix could not have been the man in the passageway. Such an action was foreign to his nature.

But, if she consented to marry him ...
She could well imagine the harsh, cutting
words that would issue from the Earl's stern
lips.

She looked up to find Mr. Felix regarding
her closely. "I – I fear that I have overdone,"
she stammered. "If you'll forgive me, I must
lie down."

"Of course, of course. I did not wish to
tire you unduly. My question will wait till
another day. Here, Milly, help Miss Duncan.
You must rest now, my dear, and you'll soon
be restored to us."

Faith nodded weakly. Her feeling of illness
was not faked. She actually felt weak at
the prospect of being confronted with Mr.
Felix's offer. "Th-thank you for coming," she
muttered.

He squeezed her hand once more and
silently departed. Faith lay in a half-daze.
All her strength seemed to have deserted her
again. Thank goodness he had not pressed her
for an answer. If he had, she hardly knew
what she would have done.

Her mind was utter chaos as she tried
to calm herself. But beads of perspiration
appeared on her forehead. She must make
some kind of a decision. For it certainly
appeared that as soon as she was recovered
he would press his suit again.

Suddenly the door that led into the next room opened and the Earl appeared. He sent Milly a stern look. "Go to the kitchen and see what needs to be done. Miss Duncan will call when she needs you."

The little maid bobbed a curtsey and moved silently from the room. There were no giggles in evidence now, thought Faith as she tried to marshal her wandering thoughts.

The Earl drew a chair up to the bed and settled himself comfortably. "My brother was here. What did he want?"

Faith stared at him in surprise. How had he known? She struggled to raise herself against the pillows. The Earl stood and helped her, his hands gentle on her shoulders. Then he reseated himself.

"What did he want?" he asked again evenly.

"He – he came to see how I was doing."

"I see." The Earl's dark brows drew together. He seemed lost in thought.

"Why did you tell them that I had a fever?" Faith asked.

He smiled grimly. "I had my reasons. I do not care to go into them."

Faith bit her bottom lip. When he spoke to her in that stern tone, she wanted to do anything to make him stop.

"What else did he say?" his lordship asked.

"Nothing." Faith felt the scarlet flooding her cheeks.

"Strange that *nothing* should make you color up like that," he observed dryly.

"I – I have been ill," she faltered, conscious that his eyes caught every nuance of expression on her face.

"Tell me the rest of what he said," commanded the Earl, fixing her with a stern eye.

For long moments Faith remained obstinately silent. It seemed wrong to betray to his lordship his brother's plan to make her an offer. "He spoke of his concern for my health," she said at last, refusing to meet his eyes. It was unfortunate that she had so little practice at lying.

"Faith," said his lordship. "You are not telling me the whole truth. You know it and I know it. Now come, what *did* Felix say to you?" His mouth curved in a wicked grin. "Did he make you a dishonorable proposition that you are afraid to repeat to me?"

"Indeed not!" Faith hurried to reply. "His offer will be honorable, I'm sure. Oh!" She realized too late how he had tricked her and she glared at him.

Her discomfort seemed to amuse him. "Did he mention the word *marriage?*"

"Of cour –" Faith stopped. "I said I was ill

and he did not finish. He spoke of a question he wished to ask me."

"And did he use the word *marriage?*" persisted his lordship.

Faith frowned. "No. But I stopped him. I – I felt I had to lie down."

"Indeed." The Earl's tone conveyed that he was aware of her stratagem. "You handled it very well. A fine lady of the *ton* could not have done better."

"I was ill," Faith asserted. "I did not *handle* anything."

The Earl grinned at her wickedly. "You are being foolish if you expect me to believe such Banbury tales. You are not ill now," he pointed out practically. "Nor were you ill before my brother arrived."

Faith pressed a hand to her forehead. "In spite of all you say I cannot believe that Mr. Felix would make me such an offer as you speak of."

The Earl shrugged. "He has certainly pulled the wool over your eyes. Dear, sweet, mild Felix. How fortunate that Aunt is not taken in by this seeming affection."

"I do not know what childhood occurrence is responsible for your hostile attitude toward your brother," Faith replied evenly. "But surely you cannot suspect him of wishing to harm your aunt."

The Earl smiled, a smile that boded ill for someone. "I have not been deceived by my brother's mild manners and meek ways," he replied with a frown. "He may not wish to harm my aunt. At the present moment it would gain him little. But he does want to convince her to change her will – in his favor. I've no doubt of that."

Faith stared at him. "How can you say such a despicable thing about your own brother?" she demanded.

"Quite easily," replied the Earl cheerfully. "After all, it's the truth."

"I don't believe you," cried Faith. "Mr. Felix is a good man – kind, gentle, good-mannered."

"Not top-lofty and arrogant like his brother, eh?" observed his lordship with a smile which Faith found excessively irritating.

"You said that, not I," she sputtered. "You are being unfair to your brother."

The Earl frowned. "I wish that were so, my dear, I truly do. But Felix is not likely to have changed this late in life."

Faith drew herself up as much as possible. "You are wasting your breath," she said firmly. "I quite refuse to believe ill of Mr. Felix."

The Earl's eyes sparkled dangerously. "Yet you are quite ready to believe it of me."

"Your actions," replied Faith stiffly, "do not always mark you as one with consideration for others."

The Earl chuckled. "No, I suppose they do not." He eyed her speculatively. "I always have been persistent. When I want something, I usually get it."

"That is not a particularly endearing quality," Faith observed irritably.

"Perhaps not," his lordship replied with another chuckle. "But *I* am rather endearing, don't you think?"

"Indeed I do not," she cried, quite forgetting her position in the household. "You are the most puffed-up, tyrannical – oh!" Suddenly becoming aware of her own words, she stopped abruptly. Whatever was she thinking of to speak to him like that!

The Earl moved from his chair to the side of the bed. "Please don't stop," he said, grinning wickedly. "It's so seldom that anyone pays me compliments."

"Oh!" Faith felt like throwing a pillow at him. "You are impossible," she cried. "Quite, quite impossible!"

"And you, my sweet," replied the Earl with that charming smile. "You are quite beautiful in your anger."

And before she could do or say a thing he had gathered her in his arms and kissed her tenderly. At first Faith struggled, but she was weak and, besides, it was difficult to win against her own body which wanted to betray her by melting into his arms.

"Milord!" she protested when he released her lips. "You must not. It is highly improper."

His only reply was to nuzzle her ear with his lips.

"Milord!" She could not stand this much longer, Faith thought, striving to push him away.

"I am a patient man," he said, with only a slight frown. "And I have several other pressing matters that must be attended to. However, do not think that I have given up on what I want. I never give up."

He brushed her lips once more lightly with his and laying her gently back among the pillows, he kissed the tip of her nose. "You must rest now and recuperate. Do you hear?"

Faith nodded numbly. She was still trying to cope with the indescribable weakness that had crept over her with that little kiss on her nose. How was it possible for such a kiss to make her feel – yes, cherished was the word.

"Excellent," said his lordship. "I expect that you will be up and about in the next several days. And," his dark eyes glittered down at her, "if my brother should come around again to make you an offer, tell him that you are considering one from me."

"Oh!" Faith felt the scarlet flood her cheeks again. "I shall do no such thing," she declared hotly. "The poor man would be quite distressed to hear such a thing."

The Earl's eyes narrowed. "Someday soon your innocence will have a rough awakening, I fear." Then he shrugged. "Be that as it may. I have done what I could to forewarn you."

As she opened her mouth to protest again, he frowned darkly. "Enough talking. You will overtire yourself and then it will be even longer until you are fit to return to your duties."

This Faith knew to be the truth although she did not particularly care to hear it from him. And so she pressed her lips together and made no comment.

"That is a sensible girl," said the Earl with another smile. And touching her cheek lightly with a finger, he left the room.

In her nest of pillows Faith sighed. How was she ever to free herself from her misplaced affection for such a man? He was everything she had told him he was: arrogant, top-lofty, tyrannical, puffed-up. But he could also be gentle and kind, almost inconceivably so. And when he touched her . . .

Faith sighed. She was not being practical

about any of this. Her illness seemed to have affected her mind. Otherwise she would surely be making plans to remove herself from the Earl's vicinity. Why, today he had gone so far as to say that he would make her an offer – dishonorable, of course. But what kind of offer could it be? He had already said he was willing to pay her three times her wages.

Faith shifted nervously in the big bed. She supposed the next time he would offer her even more money. It was not that that distressed her. She would never sell herself for any sum of money.

But how was she to combat this weakness that overcame her at his merest touch? And how was she to resist him if the time came – as it seemed likely it would – when he ignored her protests? Would she be able to stop him? And, even worse to consider – would she want to?

Chapter 15

And so several more days passed. Each day saw Faith stronger and more eager to be about her duties. And finally his lordship allowed her to resume them.

It was on the afternoon of her third full day back on her feet that he entered the room to find her stitching at yet another gown while the Countess recalled stories of her days at court.

Faith flushed when his lordship entered. His words about waiting were always on her mind. And Mr. Felix's projected offer haunted her imagination. But so far neither of them had renewed the subject.

The Earl scrutinized her carefully. "Aunt, don't you think she still looks a little pale?"

The Countess nodded, her eyes dancing with the same mischief that gleamed in her nephew's.

"I am quite well," returned Faith, intent on the sewing to which she had returned her eyes.

"*I* am the physician here," replied his lordship, "and I insist that you need some fresh air. The sun is quite warm today and a little stroll will do you good. Just in the courtyard. No moors today."

Faith suppressed a shudder. She supposed that sometime she should return to the moors. But at the present time she was afraid she just could not appreciate their beauty.

"Now, Faith," commanded the Countess. "Hugh is quite right. Fetch your cloak and go with him. I'll ring for Deevers and we'll have a cup of tea together."

"Yes, milady." Faith put aside her sewing. There was little point in arguing, she knew. Separately the Countess and her nephew could best her weak arguments. Together they would certainly win over her. In a moment she was back, her cloak over her arm and her heart pounding in her throat.

"Very good," observed his lordship with a smile to his aunt. "I'll bring her back with rosy cheeks. You shall see."

"Go on now," cried the Countess. "And leave an old woman in peace."

Faith remained silent as the Earl guided her down the stairs to the front door. As he got his own cloak from Spacks, she hastened to don hers. Having his help was too dangerous a business, too dangerous by far.

If he suspected her reasons in this, he did not indicate so. He merely took her arm and guided her out along the walk where the pine and birch seemed to be reaching upward toward the sun.

Faith took a deep breath. It was a lovely day, and it did get tiresome always being stuck indoors. In London, though she had been out in the city but little, she had always managed a few moments a day in the private courtyard of her employer.

"Faith." The Earl was staring at her.

"What? Oh, I'm sorry."

"You may as well enjoy the air while you are here," he said. "But that is not why I brought you out."

"It's not?" Faith found suddenly that her heart was thudding in her throat. She must resist him, she told herself. She simply must.

It almost seemed as though he could read her mind. "Nor am I going to make you the offer I spoke of."

"Then – then why?" asked Faith, aware of disappointment as well as relief.

"I want your help."

"In what?"

"I have devised a plan that should tell us if my estimation of my brother is false."

"What kind of plan?" asked Faith.

"I want you to let fall at the dinner table that Aunt has changed her will. That she has excluded me and left all to Felix."

"But I don't see –" Faith began.

"You don't need to see," returned the Earl. "All you need to do is trust me."

For a long moment Faith looked into those dark eyes and then she forced herself to speak. "But if what Mr. Felix says of you is true –"

"Then how can my plan hurt Aunt?" he asked, reaching out to take one of her hands in his. As always his touch weakened her, but

227

she marshaled all her wits to consider what he had asked of her. Try as she might she could not see any way that he might benefit from it. Neither did she see what he hoped to gain by it. But that, of course, was hardly necessary.

His fingers squeezed hers. "Come, Faith, you trusted me before."

She looked up at him wide-eyed.

"Did you not trust me when you walked with me? And how could you be so sure I would come for you when you were left on the moors if you did not have some trust in me? Come, Faith, say you'll help me. If my plan works, we will solve all the mysteries at once and then we can get back to the important business of living."

The look in his eyes as he said this caused the red to stain her cheeks again. What did he mean by important business? Was he referring to that "offer" he had spoken of?

"I – I –"

He squeezed her fingers again. "Please, Faith, give me this chance to prove myself to you," he begged.

"I – All right.. What do you want me to do?"

He tucked her arm through his. "First we must continue our walk. I brought you outside because that way I could be sure we were not being spied on."

Faith felt the color rush to her cheeks again at the thought that someone might have witnessed the private scenes between them.

"I see," she murmured.

"Now," continued his lordship, "this is what I want you to do. Tomorrow night at dinner – not tonight – say that Aunt has changed her will. Then congratulate Felix. If I don't miss my guess, he will be highly pleased."

"But that will not prove anything," cried Faith. "Except that he is a normal human being with normal instincts."

His lordship smiled. "You are quite right, my dear."

"Then why –" she began.

"You will have to trust me in regard to that, Faith. But I promise you, this will settle the question for you one way or another. Trust me."

He swung her around to look at him. "As you observed to me not too long ago, my sweet, my being a rake does not necessarily preclude my being trustworthy." His eyes twinkled. "At least in other matters."

"Yes, milord. I know that. I will do as you ask."

The Earl smiled, a warm, tender, somehow special smile that threatened to dissolve her bones and seemed to make her breathing difficult.

"Thank you, your trust is not misplaced," he said.

Slowly he resumed their walk and they went some paces in silence. Faith's mind was a mass of riotous thoughts. Should she really trust such a man? She had been warned against him. But he had several times saved her and the irrefutable evidence of her senses insisted that in his presence she was safe and secure.

Unconsciously she sighed. The evidence of her senses was not the most appropriate under the circumstances. Perhaps she should pay more heed to Mr. Felix's warnings about his lordship. But his lordship had also warned her about his brother. It seemed inconceivable that the round-faced, mild-mannered Mr. Felix could be guilty of anything. And yet, someone had thrown the cloak over her head and left her on the moors. Someone lean and strong – like the man whose arm she held.

Faith willed herself not to shudder. It seemed impossible to believe either of the brothers capable of wrongdoing. Yet she knew that her estimation of Mr. Felix was based on objective, observable facts, whereas that of the Earl grew out of much more subjective, emotional feelings. And it was an undeniable fact that many young women were led into disaster by their feelings. Certainly any regular reader of the *Times* would know that.

Another sigh escaped her. The Earl pressed her arm. "Hold on a little longer, my dear. Soon everything will be over."

"I sincerely hope so," declared Faith. "I am not used to living in such turmoil."

The Earl made no reply to this, but turned and began to make his way back toward the great door.

When Faith rose from dinner that evening, she was still trying to decide *how* the Earl's plan would reveal the truth. But she was no nearer to discovering that than she had been when he first broached the subject to her. She wished that she were finished with her part of the whole unpalatable thing.

Lady Clarisse had spent as much time as possible clinging to his lordship's arm and looking up at him from under lowered lashes. The lady's whole approach, thought Faith, was rather obvious, almost disgusting. How could the man stand it, she wondered, as she finished her custard. But then, perhaps the Earl found the lady amusing. She felt a certain sense of uneasiness and thrust it from her. Such thoughts, indeed *any* thoughts, about the Earl, were foolish and uncalled for.

Putting down her napkin, she prepared to rise from the table. Mr. Felix laid a detaining hand on her arm. "Miss Duncan, if I might speak to you for a moment?"

"Of course, sir." Faith could not help seeing the glance his lordship shot her way. If Mr. Felix made her an offer, she could not tell him she was considering one made by his lordship. Such a thing would be quite shocking to him.

Mr. Felix gave her his arm. "We shall use the library."

"Of course, brother." His lordship smiled coldly. "We will give you your privacy."

"Thank you." Mr. Felix seemed to ignore the Earl's sarcasm. Didn't he hear it, wondered Faith. Or did he just choose not to notice it?

As they moved off down the hall and into the library, she was also conscious of a strange look in Spacks's eyes. What did the moribund butler think of her? Certainly he must have speculations concerning a nurse-companion who was so often in the company of one brother or the other.

Mr. Felix closed the door and waved her to the divan. "Privacy is necessary in matters like this," he said as he joined her.

Faith shifted uneasily. She did not want to

upset him by refusing his offer. Yet she was far too unsure of the condition of her mind to be able to give any offer very serious consideration.

Mr. Felix took her hand in his. "For some time now I have been wanting to ask you a question," he said. "And finally I have the chance." He cleared his throat. "For some time now it has been my desire to find a wife. Not caring for the amusements of the city, I wish nothing more than to remain here and care for Aunt. You, too, I am convinced, care for her."

Faith nodded. "Yes, of course."

Mr. Felix beamed. "I wish to ask you to become my wife."

There it was, thought Faith. And he must be answered. "I – you have been most kind to me, sir. Most kind. But you see, I have not considered marriage and so I must have time to think."

"Of course. Of course. I understand." He patted her hand. "You take all the time you want, my dear. All the time you want."

Faith forced herself to smile. "You are very kind to me, sir."

As he leaned closer, she felt her heart begin to thud. And then he was kissing her. His lips were warm on hers and the kiss was like the man – mild and gentle.

Faith did not feel any response to it within herself, but neither did she feel repulsion. It was merely ordinary. So, she told herself, at least now she knew for certain that it was not the act of being kissed but the identity of the man doing it that influenced her.

She drew back just a little, suddenly aware of what life might be like for a woman who was the recipient of one man's kisses when she desired another's.

"I – the Countess expects me, sir. I will think about your kind offer, indeed I will."

"That is all I ask," said Mr. Felix with a smile. "I'm sure that serious consideration will show you the benefits of becoming my wife."

"Of course," Faith mumbled as she rose. "Now, I must go to the Countess."

There was no one about as she made her way up the great stone stairs, and Faith was very grateful. Right at that moment she did not want to meet his lordship or feel his sardonic eyes upon her. This was a time for serious thinking about her future, not for girlish speculations about a darkly handsome Earl.

But the Countess was awake and eager to talk and so Faith had little time for serious thinking.

"I am so glad you came to us," said the

Countess as Faith prepared her for bed. "But I cannot for the life of me understand how Felix found you."

"It was really quite simple," replied Faith with a smile. "He put an advertisement in the *Times* and I answered it."

The Countess shook her head. "Now if Hugh had brought you, I could understand it."

"Milady," said Faith gently "Aren't you awfully hard on Mr. Felix?"

The Countess frowned. "I suppose I am, but I never could stand him, hard as I tried. As a boy he was always whining about something and running to me with tales about his brother's misdeeds. I hate a sniveling traitor."

"Milady!" Faith had not meant for her exclamation to be so vehement, but the Countess's words had shocked her. "What an awful thing to say about your nephew."

"I'm sorry, Faith. You're a good, kindhearted creature. Too good to suspect people of evil. But I've lived in this world a lot longer."

Faith did not attempt to continue the conversation. It was certainly not her place to argue with her employer. Still, it pained her to see the old woman so cross with someone who had tried so hard to help her.

"I'm glad I answered the advertisement," said Faith. "You have been very good to me."

The Countess smiled. "You are such a delight to me after all those other ninnies. I don't know where Felix found them, but they were quite unbelievable."

As the Countess chattered on about the foibles and follies of her unfortunate predecessors, Faith found herself wondering if the Earl had pursued them, too. Well, at least both the Earl and the Countess had said that they didn't stay long. Faith stifled a sigh. Poor unfortunate girls. The world was not an easy place for a young woman on her own, of that she was quite certain.

Finally the Countess was settled to their mutual satisfaction and Faith moved softly to her own room. As she moved quietly about, removing her gown and slipping into one of her new nightdresses, her thoughts returned again and again to the Earl and his brother. Should she accept Mr. Felix's legitimate offer? An offer that meant safety and security, but that would upset the Countess and fill the Earl with sardonic amusement. But if she did not accept, wouldn't the Earl continue to pursue her? And how long could she expect to withstand him?

With a sigh Faith loosened the coil of chestnut hair and picked up her brush. Weeks

236

ago, before she had heard of Moorshead Castle, she would have laughed to scorn any suggestion that her reputation and honor might someday be in jeopardy. But now, she told herself, she was somewhat wiser. And there was no denying his lordship's charm or her attraction to him.

Absently she brushed her hair in long smooth strokes. The whole thing was much too difficult for contemplation. Everyone in this gloomy castle seemed to suspect everyone else. And all that suspicion certainly did nothing to improve dispositions, including her own.

She switched the brush to her other hand. If things had been different here . . .

If there had been only Mr. Felix – no Earl with those dark piercing eyes that seemed to read the very secrets of her soul – she might well have accepted his offer immediately. Nurse-companions to elderly ladies did not often have the opportunity to avail themselves of matrimony. And Mr. Felix was a good man. In spite of his aunt's harsh words about him, Faith had never seen him behave badly.

Or if there had been only his lordship and no mysterious goings-on to make her mistrust him . . . Involuntarily Faith exclaimed aloud. She must stop this kind of thinking. Under no circumstances would she compromise herself or her honor. No indeed.

She brought the brush down with added intensity and was startled to hear the Earl drawl, "Please do not attack such lovely hair so vehemently."

Faith swung around to face him. "Milord, am I to have no privacy?"

The Earl smiled cheerfully. "I tapped on the door and, receiving no answer, grew fearful for your safety." His words were sober enough, but his dark eyes were dancing.

"You mock me," replied Faith, conscious that she wished very much to be taken into his lordship's strong arms.

"Indeed, I do not." His eyes bored into hers. "I am greatly concerned for your safety. As you well know."

He took a step closer and Faith felt her breath quicken.

"Come, I wish to hear about my brother's discussion with you."

Faith attempted to look dignified, though she was aware that in a nightdress this was not easily accomplished. "Mr. Felix's business with me was of a private nature," she replied stiffly. "It is of no concern to you."

"On the contrary," said the Earl grimly. "It is of every concern to me. Now, what did he have to say?"

Stubbornly Faith shook her head.

"Very well, I shall wake Aunt and *she* will order you to tell me." His lordship's eyes held hers. "Come, you know she will do it. Must we disturb her rest?"

"You are grossly unfair," cried Faith angrily. "You have no right to pry into my private affairs. No right at all."

The Earl smiled cynically. "We will discuss my rights in regard to you on some other, more auspicious, occasion. But for now – do you tell me what I wish to know or do we wake Aunt?"

"Oh, very well!" Faith threw the hairbrush onto the bed with such violence that it bounced off onto the floor. Her eyes sparked as she glared at him.

"You are very beautiful in your anger," observed his lordship with that languid grin she so despised.

"And you are insulting in your curiosity," she declared, driven by her anger to lengths she would never have imagined.

"Come, we have bandied about enough words. I wish to know what he said."

Faith hesitated. It seemed so unfair to repeat their conversation.

"Did he make you an offer?"

She nodded.

"For how much?" inquired the Earl.

Faith, already infuriated by his attitude, wished momentarily that she still held the brush. She would like to throw it at him. "He offered me his good name – marriage," she said, making her tone as frosty as possible.

"Well, I'll be –" The Earl paused and frowned in bewilderment. Then he spoke again. "And what was his price?"

Faith stared at him. "You mistake yourself, milord. Mr. Felix knows that I have nothing but my wages here."

His lordship scowled darkly. "And did you accept him?"

Faith shook her head. "I – I asked him for time to think it over."

His lordship smiled. It was not a smile she liked. "You will refuse him," he said evenly.

"Milord!" Faith was past thinking coherently. How dare he interfere in her private life? Who did he think he was? "May I remind you that *I* am the one concerned here. It is my life in question. I shall think the matter over thoroughly and then come to a rational decision."

"You will refuse him," repeated the Earl obstinately.

"And if I do not?" she cried angrily.

"I shall tell him that I have had you." He said the dreadful words in such a matter-of-fact tone that for a moment they failed to register.

Then she gasped. "You lie."

"I know that," replied the Earl. "But poor Felix will not. From childhood on I could always deceive him."

"You are abominable!" cried Faith, conscious of a strong desire to flail at him with her fists.

"So I have been told," he replied cheerfully. "By many sweet young things. But that is simply part of my inestimable charm."

"I do not find you charming," declared Faith. "Indeed, you are the most arrogant, top-lofty, high-in-the-instep tyrant, I have ever seen."

"Your sampling of men, of course, has been quite limited," he replied. "But I accept the title. However, you have forgotten one other thing." His eyes held hers captive. "I always get what I want. As I said before, I am a patient man, but I do not wait forever."

Faith, her knees trembling beneath the nightdress, forced herself to meet those eyes that she so feared. "Perhaps your lordship will have to change your perception of yourself. Perhaps you have now become a man who does *not* get what he wants."

With two strides he closed the distance between them and his hands reached out to grasp her shoulders. "I have seldom waited this long for any woman, Faith Duncan. And never for one who professed to care so little for me. I hear what you say with those lovely lips; I hear your denial. But your eyes tell me quite different things. They beg me to make you mine."

"No! You are wrong!" Did her eyes really give away her innermost thoughts? she wondered. She was afraid to look at him, but she could not seem to wrench her eyes away.

She forced herself to utter a brittle laugh. "You only see in my eyes what *you* put there, milord, put there from your own foolish fancies. I suppose it's understandable that your success with the ladies of the *ton* should have gone to your head. But I am not a fashionable lady intent on acquiring, or starring in, the latest gossip. I ask only to do the job that I came here to do – to care for the Countess."

For long moments his eyes remained locked with hers. Once he leaned slightly toward her and her heart rose up in her throat at the thought that he would kiss her. But then he straightened abruptly, his hands fell from her shoulders, and he swung on his heel and strode from the room, cursing under his breath.

For some moments Faith stood where he had left her. Then, in a sort of half-daze, she made her way to the great bed and crept under the covers, there to lie restlessly until sleep came to claim her with foolish dreams of a life of peace and happiness, with the Earl by her side.

Chapter 16

The next evening as Faith prepared for dinner she considered again and again the thing his lordship had asked of her. No matter how she viewed it, it seemed that his plan could harm no one. And yet she felt uneasy about it. It seemed, no, it *was* dishonest, to tell Mr. Felix something that wasn't true. And surely he would be quite upset when he learned the real truth. And yet, she had given her word to the Earl. She knew that he depended upon her. Without her help his plan, whatever it was, would fail.

Faith sighed as she slipped into the rose-lavender dress. As always it made her think of the Earl and their first walk on the moors.

So many things had happened since then. So many things that she could not understand.

She tucked a stray wisp of hair into place and swung away from the cheval glass. By now she was getting used to the sight of herself in her new gowns. Now she no longer felt that she looked strange in them. In fact, now she felt strange in the old ones.

As she made her way down the stairs she considered how best to speak to Mr. Felix. Perhaps when he inquired about his aunt's day, as he unfailingly did, she would mention the new will. Yes, that would probably be the best.

She made her way to the dining room to find the others already gathered there. They turned to face her.

"Good evening, Miss Duncan," said Mr. Felix in his usual calm tones. "I trust Aunt is well."

Faith nodded. "Oh yes, sir. She seems quite well. In sound mind and everything."

Mr. Felix's eyes focused on her sharply. "Sound mind?"

"Yes, sir," she replied cheerfully. "Isn't that what they say when people write their wills?"

She heard the gasp from Lady Clarisse and felt rather than saw the Earl's eyes light on

244

her speculatively. "My aunt is writing a new will?" Mr. Felix asked carefully.

Faith nodded. She despised herself for tricking such a good-natured man, but she must see this through to its end. "Yes, sir. She said that the old one was no good anymore and she had me burn it in the fire." Faith found herself a little amazed at the magnitude of her lies. They seemed to come pouring out of her of their own volition.

"Aunt did not summon her lawyer," mused Mr. Felix.

The Earl snorted. "If Aunt decides something, she intends to do it immediately. That has always been the way of her. No doubt she intends to send for Travers later to formalize matters. But whatever she's done is quite legal, I collect. Aunt never does things by halves."

His dark eyes met Faith's momentarily and she felt a warmth inside her.

Lady Clarisse, as usual hanging on the Earl's arm, had finally regained her breath. "I suppose she wanted to include *you*," she told Faith acidly.

Faith thought quickly. That certainly seemed a likelihood if the Countess had really written a new will. She nodded. "Yes, milady, she was most generous, I believe." Her eyes went to Mr. Felix. "But the bulk of her personal wealth – well, she said she had misjudged Mr. Felix and wanted to make amends to him."

Lady Clarisse laughed brittly. "I'm not so sure about the sound mind."

Mr. Felix eyed her reproachfully. "I am sorry, Lady Clarisse, that Aunt did not see fit to leave you something, but after all, it *is* her money."

"Of course it is," said the lady, evidently regretting her breach of etiquette. "And I need for nothing. My late husband left me quite well provided for."

Neither of the gentlemen made reply to this and Faith wondered idly how Lady Clarisse would behave if she knew that everyone in the room was aware of the precarious state of her finances and of her machinations to acquire more money. Would she, for instance, still hang so sweetly on the Earl's arm and look up at him so adoringly if she knew that he was merely toying with her?

There was no answer to such a question and Faith put her hand on the arm that Mr. Felix offered her and allowed him to lead her to the table. Mr. Felix smiled expansively as he seated her. It was easy to see that he was pleased with the fiction that she had fed him. But surely that was natural. After all, he had been most kind to his aunt and

246

this was not merely a question of money. The act of changing her will would certainly mean that the Countess had changed her mind about him. And that would surely be a matter of joy to a conscientious man like Mr. Felix.

As the dinner progressed, she managed to fill her plate and empty it, but she had little idea of what she was eating. Her thoughts were centered on the Earl's plan. He had obviously been pleased at the way she had played her part. That swift look of his had told her that as sure as words. But now what? What did he expect to accomplish by her convincing Mr. Felix that his aunt had forgiven him?

Lady Clarisse was more silent than usual and Faith had nothing more to say. She had done her part and now she wished she had not. Never in her life had she told so many lies. Lie after lie, they had followed one another so smoothly from her lips. And all these years she had considered herself a decent, upright woman. She had never lied in her other positions – not even to protect herself from a scolding. But since she had come to Moorshead, everything had changed.

The brothers did not seem to notice how little the women contributed to the conversation. Cheerfully, they talked about everyday matters, almost, thought Faith with a start, as though they were, and always had been, on equitable terms.

After dessert she put down her napkin and prepared to push back her chair.

Mr. Felix smiled at her. "I know you are anxious to return to Aunt. But before you do, will you have a little brandy with us? After all, the day has been a fortunate one for you, too."

Faith nodded, carefully keeping her face calm. It seemed somehow wrong to think of this as a fortunate day. Even if the story had been true, she somehow could not think it fortunate to be mentioned in someone's will. It seemed indecent, somehow, that she should rejoice over money that could only be hers through someone else's death.

"Let us have our brandy in the library," suggested Mr. Felix. "I have a special bottle put away. I will go get it, Hugh, if you will escort the ladies?"

The Earl nodded. "Of course."

Mr. Felix turned back to the butler. "Some glasses, Spacks."

Spacks nodded. "Yes, sir. Right away, sir."

It was strange, thought Faith, how people of quality spoke before their servants of such private things. It was almost as though they believed that the servants were another species, unable to understand what they heard. But Spacks had heard, she was quite sure. And in minutes every servant in the castle would have heard everything that went on in the dining room, and perhaps more.

The Earl approached and offered her his arm. Lady Clarisse frowned at him. "I don't see how you can be so calm, Hugh. He's going to get what should be yours."

The Earl shrugged. "It's only money."

For a moment Lady Clarisse stared at him as though he had lost his senses. And then she smiled. "Of course, Hugh dear. How silly of me. You're quite right. It's only money." And she took the Earl's other arm.

Faith, pacing sedately by his lordship's side to the library, marveled at how transparent Lady Clarisse had become. Didn't she realize how clearly those around her could read her mercenary motives? Oh well, Faith dismissed the lady from her mind.

That was really not a difficult task; all she had to do was let herself become aware of the nearness of the Earl. It was quite disturbing to be so close to him. It seemed somehow to interfere with her ability to breathe.

The Earl seated her before the fire and, settling the Lady Clarisse on a divan, dropped down casually beside her. Faith was conscious of something very like jealousy within herself. How foolish, she thought, to let herself be disturbed because his lordship seated himself beside the lady. He would hardly announce his preference for Faith in front of the others. *If* he had such a preference, she told herself sternly.

Her thoughts were interrupted by Mr. Felix, who entered carrying a tray with glasses and a partially filled bottle of brandy. He set the tray on a nearby table and handed Faith a half-filled glass.

"It is very potent, this brandy, so sip carefully. You may even want to take it back to your room. I know how conscientious you are about your duties."

As he handed about the other glasses, Faith took a tentative sip. She had never drunk spirits before, her former employers believing that a servant who was supplied with tea could count herself fortunate. But even the very small sip that Faith managed was too much. The fiery liquid seemed to burn the lining of her throat on its way down. Tears stood out in her eyes and she fought down the desire to cough. Somehow she had thought that the drink would be more pleasant.

The Earl, however, noticed her difficulty. He smiled as he sniffed the aroma from his glass and then sipped daintily. "I think your suggestion was quite to the point, Felix. Miss Duncan would do well to take her glass back with her. If you will excuse me momentarily, I will escort her back upstairs. I wish to have a word with Aunt."

Mr. Felix's forehead wrinkled into a frown, but before he could speak, his lordship laughed dryly. "I should not worry, if I were you," he said. "Of all persons you are in the best position to know that nothing and no one can change Aunt's mind. Besides, it is of another matter that I wish to speak to her."

Clearly Mr. Felix did not believe this, but he said no more and the Earl, setting down his glass, rose and offered Faith his arm. "I shall carry your glass, too," he said, his fingers brushing hers as he removed it from her grasp.

Faith's knees trembled as she rose and took his arm. "Goodnight," she said to Mr. Felix. He nodded. "Goodnight, milady."

"Goodnight." Lady Clarisse was obviously trying to keep her irritation under control, but it was clear that she was annoyed by his lordship's defection.

He smiled at her cheerfully. "Do your best to keep Felix company, my dear Clarisse. Behave in your usual witty fashion. That will captivate him."

Lady Clarisse shot his lordship a look of suppressed fury which quite startled Faith.

But Mr. Felix simply shook his head and looked mildly reproving.

"They are well suited to keep each other company," observed his lordship softly as they reached the great hall.

"What?" Faith turned startled eyes to him. "How can you put Mr. Felix in the same class with *that* woman?"

The Earl chuckled. "Your claws are showing, my dear. I assure you that Felix and Clarisse are two of a kind, but I know you will not believe me."

He paused before the door of her room and lowered his voice. "Listen to me carefully. I want you to go to bed early. And whatever transpires I want you to stay there. Do you understand?"

"But the Countess? I have my duties."

"Do not worry about that. The Countess will be well provided for. I want you to get into your nightdress, get into your bed, and drink the rest of your brandy. It will help you sleep. Do you understand?"

His dark eyes gazed into hers. "Yes, milord. I understand."

"Good. Now I will go and tell Aunt what has happened. She will not expect you anymore tonight." He bent and dropped a kiss on her forehead. "Sleep well."

"Goodnight, milord." She watched him

make his way through the door to the Countess's room. Then she dropped into a chair.

The Earl expected something to happen tonight, expected it or *planned* it. And he wanted her out of the way. Faith sighed. She could not do as his lordship had told her. She must stay awake and guard the Countess. That was her duty.

She had done as his lordship asked in telling his lie, but she could not be sure that he was entirely trustworthy. The evidence of her senses might be sufficient if only her own life were at stake, as when they had walked on the moor. But that was not the case now. She must not allow anything to happen to the Countess.

She considered. She would wait in the semi-darkness of the Countess's room. Wait and see exactly what his lordship was up to. Absently she reached for the brandy glass and sipped.

It was sometime later, when Faith heard the sound of the door to the hall closing. Softly she crept to the door that led to the next room. The room was shrouded in darkness, its familiar contours distorted by dark shadows. Faith shivered, but she dared not light a candle. What if she had misjudged the Earl? What if he meant to harm his aunt?

The thought so frightened her that she almost ran to the bed to check on the Countess. But just then through the darkness came the unmistakable sound of the Countess's breathing, the even breath of a sleeper.

Faith swallowed an hysterical giggle. How foolish she was. Softly she crept into the room, feeling her way as she went. She chose a chair back away from the fireplace, one from which she could see the fireplace but also in which she could not be seen by someone from the passageway.

Carefully she settled herself into the chair. For the first time in some minutes she realized that she still held the brandy glass. She raised it to her lips and took another sip.

Brandy, she mused, did not taste as good as she had thought it would, but then, perhaps many things in life were like that. Perhaps having a husband, perhaps even being a lady, would not be nearly so nice as one might imagine. She, of course, had never been so foolish as to imagine herself as a lady. Having good blood was not enough to get one that sort of life. A dowry was an absolute necessity.

Life with Mr. Felix would not be full of excitement, she continued, but perhaps she should consider it. It might be rather pleasant.

A strange warmth was spreading over Faith's limbs. Too late she recalled his lordship's words about the brandy helping her sleep. But certainly she had not had that much.

She moved carefully in the chair, setting down the glass, silently flexing her fingers, moving her head, shifting her eyes around the dark room. But all her efforts were of little avail. A curious lassitude seemed to be spreading over her. She felt very good, very elated in a quiet way. She knew why she was sitting here in the darkness keeping guard over the Countess, but she felt that her previous fears had been ill-founded and silly. It was ridiculous to distrust the Earl. Right now she should be sleeping in her nice comfortable bed, just as the Earl had told her to do.

Faith considered going to that bed, but her limbs seemed far too heavy to move. Her eyelids fell shut as her head lolled back against the chair and the sweetest of slumbers overtook her.

Sometime later a sound in the darkened room brought her back to the edge of consciousness. With great effort she opened her eyes. She knew instantly that something was wrong with her. That sweet lassitude must have come from something stronger than the brandy. And then she heard again the sound that had wakened her – it was the sound of the fireplace opening.

Through half-raised eyelids she made out the form of a dark figure as it glided from the passageway. Without looking around, it moved confidently toward the big bed.

As the intruder drew close to the bed Faith tried to scream, to spring from the chair, and rush to the Countess's aid. But her tongue and her limbs seemed paralyzed. She was unable to move or make a sound.

Dear God, thought Faith, as the dark figure neared the bed, her brandy had been drugged. While he was carrying it upstairs, the Earl had dropped something into it! She had trusted the wrong man and now the Countess would die. She tried again to rise from the chair but was unsuccessful.

And then, just as the dark figure leaned over the bed, an arm seemed to reach out from the covers and grab it. As the two figures struggled silently there on the bed, Faith managed finally to get to her feet.

She had just attained this position and was leaning in the shadows against the wall when another figure emerged from the passageway.

A whiff of heavy scent came to Faith's nostrils. Lady Clarisse! She was part of this.

To Faith's befuddled mind it was not clear how the weakened Countess could still be struggling with the intruder. But certainly Lady Clarisse must be stopped.

As the lady stepped out from the fireplace toward the bed, Faith forced herself to move. It was beyond her strength to walk. But she could fall. And so, as Clarisse moved within reach, Faith threw herself toward her, hands outstretched. Her grasping fingers caught the back of the lady's gown and she clung to it as she went crashing to the floor, bringing the other woman with her.

The silence of the room was broken by curses as Lady Clarisse fought to free herself. Faith could not fight back, but she clung tenaciously to the gown. Her one thought was to keep Clarisse from reaching the bed.

Just as she was going to be sucked into the darkness that wanted to swallow her, she felt the gown pulled from her fingers. Then darkness descended again.

When Faith regained consciousness, someone was picking her up, carrying her to a chair. With great effort she opened her eyes, to see the Earl staring down at her.

"No." She tried to speak but could not. And then she saw that the room was lit and the Earl wore a white shirt and light buckskins. He was not dressed in black. He could not be the intruder!

"Faith, Faith," he was saying. "You must wake up. Come, you mustn't sleep."

"Stand her up," came the Countess's voice, crisp as ever.

Faith felt the relief well up in waves as the Earl pulled her to her feet.

"We must walk you, Faith. Come, I shall tell you what happened." With his arm around her, she managed to put one foot carefully before the other. The effects of the drug seemed to be wearing off.

"You should have listened to me," said the Earl as they neared the far corner of the room.

"Now Hugh," said the Countess from a great chair where she sat ensconced in pillows. "I told you she wouldn't do that. She's too conscientious."

"Yes, but I didn't think about them drugging her brandy."

"Tell me." Faith managed to get the words out.

"Clarisse and Felix were in it together. Clarisse played the ghost. That was to frighten you and keep you out of their way. It was her groom whom you followed into the tunnel. It was he who left you on the moors."

Faith shuddered. "But you said Mr. Felix?"

"I cannot blame you for not suspecting him. Felix is a past master at deception, as I learned long ago to my regret. How often I paid his gambling debts and placated his forsaken doxies on his promise that he would reform. How often he swore to my father that he led a life of innocent purity." He sighed. "With my father he could never win. Perhaps it was because his birth caused our mother's death; at any rate, our father could not stand the sight of him. And so Felix had no one to come to but me." He shook his head. "I was too young and too gullible. For many years I believed that he had been deceived and cozened, that he was the victim instead of the victimizer. But finally I was forced to realize the truth. Then I refused to stand for his debts any longer."

Faith could hardly believe her ears. "Those things you said – He really did gamble and – and keep fancy women?"

The Earl nodded grimly. "He did indeed. That round babyface makes him look so innocent, but he is not."

"No wonder you suspected me," murmured Faith.

The Earl's face hardened. "I saw you – that first evening – in his arms."

"In his arms? But I couldn't have – Oh!" Her memory of that night came flooding back. "You were just leaving. But it wasn't what you thought." The color stained her cheeks. "I tripped and he caught me."

His lordship smoothed the hair on her forehead tenderly. "You can see why I could not believe your innocence." He smiled ruefully. "For a man who prides himself on knowing women I have been unforgivably obtuse. I did not understand you and I did not suspect Clarisse at all. She played her part well. Her actions with me were merely diversionary tactics. It was she who insisted that Felix smother Aunt. So that he would be implicated and in her power."

Suddenly it all came clear to Faith. "You *thought* they would try to kill the Countess."

The Earl nodded. "I thought someone might. That's why I wanted you safely out of the way. In the darkness I closed the outer door and crept back to hide in the bed."

"But the Countess?" asked Faith.

"I didn't think Felix would risk a light so I carried her here to this chair. From here she could hear everything."

The Countess laughed harshly. "I certainly heard plenty. The curses they heaped on each other when they realized it was all up were quite eloquent."

"You were unconscious then," said the Earl.

"But where are they now?" asked Faith.

"They are locked up. With Hugh's groom on guard," declared the old lady crisply. "I do not like the scandal of bringing the magistrate into this. But it must be done. I cannot let them go free to perpetrate their wickedness on someone else." She shook her head sadly. "How their greed has undone them."

Faith sighed. Her mind still found it difficult to grasp everything. She looked up at the man whose arm supported her and her eyes filled with sudden tears. How unfair she had been to him!

"I knew that Felix had led you to mistrust me." The Earl smiled ruefully. "And my reputation as a rake did not help."

"I'm sorry," murmured Faith. She would have to leave Moorshead, she thought regretfully. For now she knew that she could not forestall the Earl forever. Her love for him was too strong.

The Earl shrugged. "Your suspicion was natural. In a way it made it easier for me to flush out Felix. But in another way it made things most difficult for me."

"I do not understand."

"Some days ago I spoke of making you an offer –"

Faith expected some sound of objection from the Countess, but none was forthcoming.

"I could not do so while you were suspicious of me."

"For mercy sakes," cried the Countess. "Don't be so long about it, Hugh."

Faith thought that her mind must still be dazed from the drug. Certainly the Countess did not expect her to accept such an offer – to become his lordship's inamorata?

"Yes, Aunt, but I find it is not an easy thing to do. I have never done it like this before."

"Then do it now."

The Earl tilted Faith's head back so that her eyes met his. "Faith, my love, will you be my –"

The tears spilled over her eyes as she realized how much she loved him. And yet, if she gave in, how would she ever respect herself again?

"Wife?" concluded his lordship.

Faith's knees failed suddenly. "Wife?" she whispered.

"Of course. Oh!" The Earl frowned. "You thought my offer would be of another kind?"

Faith could only nod.

"That was certainly wise of her," said the Countess crisply. "Especially since she thought she was dowerless."

"I *am* without a dowry," said Faith. She forced herself to continue. "I am quite below your touch, milord. But – but thank you for the compliment."

"I have never asked any woman to marry me before. Really, Aunt, it is most ironic that my first honorable offer should be refused when all my dishonorable ones were not."

"You did not ask her if she loves you," said the old woman.

"Milady!" Faith protested.

But the Earl's hand under her chin forced her to look into his eyes. "*Do* you love me?" he asked.

For one wild moment Faith thought to lie, but that would be useless, she knew. The secret of her heart was written plainly in her eyes. "Yes," she said softly. "And that is why I must leave here so that you may marry someone more fit."

"Would an heiress worth 50,000 pounds be fit?" inquired the Countess.

"Of course, milady," replied Faith, trying not to choke on her tears. It was entirely fitting that the Countess should want her nephew to marry well.

"Oh, Hugh, bring her closer. I want to see her face when I tell her the name of your bride-to-be."

It was not like the Countess to be so cruel,

thought Faith, as his lordship led her closer to the chair.

"I have in mind a girl for Hugh, a good decent girl that will make him a fine wife."

Faith nodded.

"And she is worth 50,000 pounds."

Faith nodded again, unable to say anything over the lump in her throat.

"There *was* a new will," said the Earl gently. "It names you as Aunt's heiress."

"Me?"

The Countess nodded, her bright eyes gleaming. "I knew you were right for Hugh. That's why I told him to keep away from you. He always did like a challenge."

"But —" Faith's mind was whirling.

"You needn't make any more protests," said the Countess. "They are entirely useless. I have made up my mind. Of course, you will have to live here at Moorshead."

For Faith no news could be more welcome, but she raised her eyes to the Earl's. "But won't you miss the city life?"

His lordship shrugged. "The life of a rake is highly overtouted. I shall be grateful to retire."

"And now, Hugh," cried the Countess, "will you kiss the girl so we can all get some rest?"

And there, while the Countess watched in

quiet appreciation, the Earl gathered Faith in his arms. And the kiss that he gave her then – tender and yet passionate – promised great things for their future together, great things indeed.

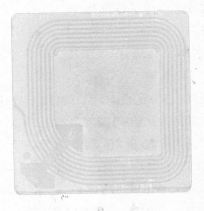